HUMAN
SPIRITUAL POWERS

JAMES L. CANNON

<u>Abstract</u>

Join Carter and Warden as they embark on a spiritual quest to discover the functional principles, laws and powers of the human soul. It is your destiny, the great Archangel Michael told them, to find and reveal for all humanity, the answers to the six epic questions:

1. WHAT IS THE MEANING OF HUMAN LIFE ON EARTH?

2. ARE HUMANS ETERNAL SOULS TRAPPED IN BODIES?

3. **WHAT SPIRITUAL POWERS DO HUMANS POSSESS?**

4. WHY ARE THERE, PAIN, SUFFERING, AND SICKNESS IN THE LIFE OF EVERY HUMAN BEING?

5. IS THERE A PARTICULAR WAY MODERN HUMANS SHOULD LIVE?

6. WHAT IS THE MEANING OF DEATH?

Each book in the series involves the answer to one of these questions with which our soul searchers create a modern **non-fiction Handbook of the Soul.** The handbook contains fascinating insights into the soul and the meaning and purpose of human life.

Thousands of years of global philosophy, theology and science have been examined to find the credible purpose and meaning of human existence. Although the fictional stories surrounding it will entertain you, the handbook's real and rational answers to the timeless questions can help you see the true nature of your soul and the meaning of human life on earth.

Acclaim for the Series

Living as a Modern Soul in a Human Body

An author with an exceptional variety of life experiences has created an exciting series of short books addressing the fundamental questions of human existence.

Viewing life from the unique perspectives of a retired university vice president, a small city mayor, a corporate manager, an undercover intelligence operative, and a decorated military officer, Mr. Cannon provides a concise and thought-provoking account of the essential elements of wisdom necessary for us to thrive and grow.

The six stories, cover life's meaning, the keys to human happiness, and spiritual powers we can all claim, as well as the purpose of virtue, and morality. They also cover ways to encounter God, experience death and how to live well and die well.

The entertaining, six-book series-**Living as a Modern Soul in a Human Body**-was created to pass a very practical and valuable body of moral, ethical and spiritual knowledge to future generations. However, I heartily recommend the series as a great and easy read for anyone interested in becoming all they can be while on this Earth.

Jerry L. Beasley
President Emeritus
Concord University

Table of Contents

Book 3

HUMAN SPIRITUAL POWERS

Series

The six books included in the serial series *Living as a Modern Soul in a Human Body* are for reading in the following order:

Book 1: *The Meaning of Life*

Book 2: *Souls Trapped in Bodies*

Book 3: *Human Spiritual Powers*

Book 4: *Why Human Suffering*

Book 5: *A Soul's Code of Conduct*

Book 6: *The Meaning of Death*

HUMAN
SPIRITUAL POWERS

Book 3 in the Series

Living as a
Modern Soul in a Human Body

JAMES L. CANNON

Copyright © 2000, 2023 by James L. Cannon

Printed in the United States of America

ISBN-13:978-0-9968528-5-2

This book is dedicated to my daughter

Casey Alexandria Wright

Scriptural verses from KJV

On the cover:
Renaissance genius Leonardo da Vinci's famous 1490 drawing the Vitruvian Man (soul and apron added). With the body as the temple of the soul, da Vinci shows that there is great harmony in the symmetrical relation of the human body's parts to the whole. The body's proportions extend to the circumference of a perfect circle with its center at the navel and a perfect square when centered at the groin.

Introduction

This is the 3rd book in a serial set of six books; this book covers eternal spiritual laws, principles and the spiritual powers of the human soul plus the importance of good citizenship. If you are pressing forward with the maturity of your soul, this material should prove helpful.

The books in this series use an adventure story to convey vital spiritual truths about the nature and purpose of the human soul. Those truths are outlined in the Handbook of the Soul section of each chapter.

For clarity, **important points and concepts** are **repeated** and **expanded** from chapter to chapter. The spiritual intelligence in the Handbook of the Soul is presented in a bulleted outline format of thought-sized bites for easier reading. A glossary of terms used in this set of stories is located at the end of Book 1, and the bibliography is located at the back of Books 1 and 6.

While acknowledging many and varied sources of information, it is the author who ultimately responsible for the content, and it is my earnest hope that these pages will help make life a little more meaningful for those whose eyes may chance upon them.

James L. Cannon
Soulsline9@gmail.com
31 January 2020

Spiritual power is our greatest underdeveloped power.
...Electricity inventor Thomas A. Edison

Chapter 1

The Soul of a Good Citizen

Yelling and jeering, an APOLLYON gang is surrounding me at dusk in a clearing just outside the city where I'm headed. They are taunting me and jabbing at me with clubs and knives. I am defending myself with my walking staff, when I feel a thud and a sharp pain as a rock hits my forehead. I land a solid side kick to the ribs of one tormentor and an elbow to the jaw of another. "Thank God for my Karate training with the Ascetics, even so, I could sure use some help right about now."

The black clad gangsters are circling just out of reach, when one rushes in and grabs the end of my staff; I drop him with a left sweep and knock his breath out with the staff to the solar plexus. Looks like ten of them, with maybe eight still in the fight. A front snap kick to the groin puts down another and a spinning back kick takes out one advancing behind me." Blood from my head wound is getting in my eyes, but I must keep them off my back."

They are rushing me now; I am punching into a sea of faces. Uhh, a heavy thud strikes the back of my skull, everything is spinning; I'm down; they're kicking me hard. I'm blacking out.

About midnight when he regains consciousness, Carter realizes he has been beaten and robbed. His head hurts something awful; his wallet is empty and his clothes are torn and dirty. The good news is that his backpack, staff and journal are scattered nearby apparently of no use to the gang that attacked him.

"I better get to a doctor to make sure I'm not seriously injured," he thinks. Focusing his mind back on his mission, Carter recalls recently studying human happiness with his grandfather. They had become satisfied that they knew, in an academic sense at least, most of what was known to mankind about human happiness.

Thus armed, Carter had set forth to find his soul in the simple pleasures of the average human life. He had decided to try his luck in a big city. He was nearing the city when he was assaulted and robbed by APOLLYON. "My search for happiness has gotten off to a bad start," he's thinking when a car pulls over and a man offers him a ride.

The elderly driver says, "You are looking pretty rough son; where are you going?"

"The closest emergency room would be great," responds Carter.

The next day, he is back on his way with bruised ribs a few stitches and a mild concussion. The doctor told him his excellent physical condition probably saved him from more serious injury.

By now, he has learned somethings about the human soul, its nature, composition and disposition. He knows he is an eternal soul trapped in a human body for the duration of his time on earth, and he feels that he understands the basic meaning of human life on this planet.

In a sense, he knows that he is his soul, however, he has never fully understood enough about that critical core of himself, his true self, maybe because he has tried to capture it in a net of thought. Carter has concluded that perhaps he is trying too hard, and that a greater realization of his soul lay somewhere in happiness and in the simple pleasures of human existence.

He wants to understand more about the workings of his soul, like its operating laws, the principles of spiritual being that must make it function and most especially the spiritual powers that it may command. He believes understanding these things might help him get into more direct contact with the spiritual center of his soul. He is, therefore, seeking answers to the third great question of the spiritual quest:

WHAT SPIRITUAL POWERS DO HUMANS POSSESS?

Chapter 1 Soul of a Good Citizen

Carter stops at the entrance to a building and notices a couple of elegant women leaving for work with their briefcases. They are both of a generation earlier than his, but with beautiful and intelligent faces. They are attired in expensive professional clothing, and he thinks that perhaps they are of some importance in the community.

Carter asks the next person he encounters about the building and the names of the women who live or work there. He is told that this is the residence of a state senator who has been appointed by the governor to fill the unexpired term of her deceased husband who had been murdered the previous year.

The senator's name is Brenda, and she lives with her sister-in-law Carolyn who is an economic development director for the region. When late in the afternoon the beautiful senator returns home, Carter is standing near the entrance to her residence. She asks if she can help him.

Carter introduces himself explaining that he is a college graduate who left home to become a spiritual pilgrim, and who has been an Ascetic for the past four years. "But now," said Carter, "I have left that path and am here to make a new life in the city. Unfortunately, I was attacked and robbed last night by a gang, but I think I am OK now. Other than being broke, in bloody, torn up clothes," he adds.

Carter goes on to say, "My father suggested I meet a person of influence who might help me get started, and to be honest, you are the most beautiful person of influence I have ever seen."

At this, the senator laughed aloud, and said, "Please call me Brenda. I have never met a spiritual pilgrim that wanted to learn anything from me. But come inside and perhaps we can come to an understanding, for I have always wanted to learn of the impressive spiritual seekers."

Brenda feels an immediate connection with Carter as her husband was killed in a similar gang attack the previous year. Once inside she gives him a place to clean up and offers him some of her late husband's business clothes that fit him perfectly.

They talk at length about one another's interests in life and the qualifications Carter has for employment. Brenda suggests Carter stay with her and her sister-in-law in their guest room until they could help find him employment.

The next day, Brenda is glad to see Carter looking so trim, fit and professional in her husband's clothes. "Things are working out well," she called out to him. "We have an economic development meeting here Friday and dinner after the meeting. Carolyn and I will introduce you to a number of important employers in our community."

Carter thanks her, and when Brenda finds out that he hasn't eaten anything for a couple of days, she makes lunch, and they talk some more. Her sister-in-law Carolyn comes in and joins the conversation.

Brenda shares her goals in life and the great sorrow of losing her husband to an APOLLYON gang like the one that attacked Carter. Her husband, Jim, was killed trying to stop the gang from assaulting the pastor of their church.

Tearing up, she says, "I don't think they intended to kill him, but as usual with APOLLYON things got out of hand. I have long been seeking faith, but thus far I have been unable to find it. Now, I am busy carrying out the duties of a state senator.

"What of faith and the soul have you learned so far on your quest, my pilgrim friend?" She asks.

"Along with my Grandfather and my best friend Warden," Carter replies, "We have kept a journal of the things we have learned thus far about the human soul and the meaning of life. I would be happy to share it with you if you like."

"Oh, please do!" says Brenda with enthusiasm. "I would love to know what such self-sacrifice and fasting has taught you over a period of so many years."

"That goes for me as well," says Carolyn.

Carter explains who Warden is and how they met Dr. Moses of whom the women had heard many things. The three of them seem to enjoy one another's company, and Carter agrees to be a sort of spiritual guide in return for help in the worldly realm of business.

Chapter 1 Soul of a Good Citizen

On Friday, Carter joins them for a dinner meeting on economic development. There, he meets successful members of the business community including Myles who runs a youth recreation center, Beverly who is in the vending machine business and Carolyn's husband Mr. Bell who runs a food distribution company with his partner and attorney Mr. Cannon who is, in addition, the local Chamber of Commerce President.

Also, present, is a retired baseball coach and now big game hunting guide Bill Bryan; local sports hero Ashley the B-1 Bomber; plus, Brittany and Ryan who are in the medical field. Mrs. Palmer represents the newspaper and Mrs. Frierson runs a local motel and is a member of the county court.

The conversation centers on economic development, business and politics with sports and a few tall tales about hunting expeditions thrown in by Bill, who, recognizing Carter as a fellow outdoorsman, takes an instant liking to him.

In the evenings that follow, Carter shares his journal with Brenda and Carolyn, and they talk about things late into the nights, for both women are willing students of the spiritual with plenty of questions, comments and insights.

They also discuss the community development issues Brenda and Carolyn are dealing with including the need for more jobs and better economic policy, and especially the increasing need for better citizenship, which could help lower the crime rate.

Carter recalls that good citizenship is an important aspect of the meaning of life because it helps people live in right relationship with one another.

Eventually, they decide to collaborate on the following pages of the journal, which contain a Citizens Code of Conduct, the Rights and Responsibilities of Citizens, and the importance of a few good manners. All of which can help people live more in right relationship with one another.

"Bad officials are the ones elected by good citizens who do not vote."
...George Jean Nathan

Handbook of the Soul

A Citizens Contract

I. Preview

Social Contract - The vital social contract that makes a democracy work is the agreement that we will all be governed equally according to the laws we establish.

- ***Illegal Conduct** – Behavior considered so detrimental to society that it is prohibited by law.*

- ***Immoral Conduct** – Behavior violating a society's concepts of good and decent (moral) activity.*

- **Other Standards of Conduct** – *Various other behaviors considered unacceptable in most societies.*

- **Rights** - *Basic rights and fundamental freedoms to which each human being is entitled.*

- **Responsibilities** - *To deserve a citizen's rights, you must accept a citizen's responsibilities and duties.*

- **Manners** - *Guidelines for interpersonal behavior are known as good manners or courtesy.*

II. Introduction

Social Contract - *"The vital social contract that makes a democracy work is the agreement that we will all be governed by **laws** that are established by our elected representatives. Each of us gives up some personal freedom in order to achieve collective benefits of order, economic stability, personal safety and justice."*[1]

Strife and Discord - *In addition to legal constraints there is a general understanding that citizens should treat one another fairly and that we should try to behave in honorable ways in order to reduce significantly the level of strife and discord among us.*

Consensus of Standards - *There is no international moral or ethical code of behavior other than the criminal and civil codes in each country for illegal activity. There is, however, a certain overlapping consensus of standards among modern societies for fair and honorable behavior that, taken together, might constitute a **General Code of Human Conduct** as listed below.*

Decent Citizen - *In the management of your personal relationships, and in the course of your business and social affairs, you are expected, as a decent citizen of the human race, to conduct yourself in accordance with **at least** the following generally accepted standards of lawful, moral and ethical human behavior:*

> **The first requisite of good citizens in this republic of ours is that they shall be able and willing to pull their own weight.**
> *...26th U.S. President Theodore Roosevelt*

III. General Code of Human Conduct

A. Illegal Conduct

1. **Do no harm**:

    a. **Murder** - *Intentionally **killing** another human being is unlawful except in self-defense, in defense of your family or due to lawful military or judicial orders. Murder is illegal in all societies*

    b. **Physical Injury or Assault** – *Intentionally injuring other people is unacceptable and illegal.*

    c. **Cannibalism** - *Eating human flesh is prohibited except when absolutely necessary for survival in the most extreme circumstances.*

    d. **Rape** - *Sexual activity of any kind forced on another being is immoral, unacceptable and illegal.*

2. **Trespass** - *Trespassing on the property of others without their permission or damaging their property is wrong and generally illegal. Other people and their property should be treated with respect.*

3. **Theft** - *Stealing or extorting the property or ideas of other people is unethical and unacceptable.*

    - *"If anyone enriches himself with what is not his own, he has contracted a debt that has to be paid, whether he knows it or not."[2]*

    - *Theft is illegal in all societies.*

4. **Lying, Cheating, Deception and Fraud** - *These are unethical and dishonorable forms of human behavior.*

    - *A person's word should be good; a promise made should be a promise kept.*

    - *Debts should be paid in accordance with their terms.*

    - *Fraud, which is conducting activity for gain by deliberate deception, is generally illegal.*

5. **Legal Obligations** - *Human beings are obligated to obey all the **civil and criminal laws** of the societies in which they choose to live.*

6. **Animal Abuse** – *Abuse of animals is disgraceful and immoral, and they should be harmed or killed only for food, in self-defense or for the legitimate advancement of science and medicine.*

   - *The day will come when you are held accountable to a higher power for the way you treated those in your care including your pets.*

   - *In many societies, animal abuse is illegal.*

B. Immoral Conduct

1. **Hatred and Envy** - *Human beings should try to care as much about others as themselves, and we should not **hate or envy** anyone.*

   - *We should desire no one else's property.*

   - *We should put down our jealousy when it arises.*

2. **Adultery** - *It is immoral and dishonorable for anyone to have a sexual affair with the spouse of another person. It is a very serious breach of marriage vows for married people to have sex with anyone other than their spouses, and it greatly degrades the souls of those who do so.*

3. *__Sexual Immorality, Impurity and Debauchery__ - Prostitution, indiscriminate fornication, random sex with multiple partners, sexual affairs with children, near kin or animals has generally been considered disgraceful, perverted or illegal in most societies. In every kind of sexual immorality, there enters a coldness into the soul. It is a conscious and voluntary abuse of pleasure reserved for the marriage commitment that otherwise weakens will power, discipline and spiritual strength.*

3. **Emotional Harm** - *Inflicting intentional emotional harm on another human being is unacceptable.*

4. **Using Others** - *Using other people to advance your own selfish interests without regard for their interests is wrong.*

   - *You should treat other people the way you wish to be treated and not merely as a means of getting what you want.*

   - *The best result is known as a win-win situation where everyone involved in an activity gain something from it and is better off than they were before.*

C. Other Standards of Conduct

1. **Suicide** - *The most desperate and extreme act of despair is generally seen (with certain exceptions) as a spiritually unacceptable way out of life's challenges.*

2. **Fits of Rage** – *We must control our tempers and let not anger and rage cause us to give up actual control of our beings. A wild, violent, cursing and swearing human being that is out of control is a shameful sight and is not fit to be in the company of decent people.*

3. **Negativity and Strife** – *Most humans have enough challenges without having to put up with negativity and discord from others. The authors of such conflict and friction are usually unwelcomed acquaintances.*

4. **Self-support** - *People are expected to be responsible to work hard enough to* **support themselves and their families**; *when necessary, they should aid and assist other people who may be in* **legitimate** *need of assistance.*

5. **Golden Rule** – *Treat people the way you would like to be treated and bring misery and slander on no one.*

While we are zealously performing the duties of good citizens and soldiers, we certainly ought not to be inattentive to the higher duties of faith.
...1st U.S. President George Washington

6. **Love** and **Respect** - *Parents should **treat** their **children fairly** and **equally**, and children should treat their parents with love and respect. All human beings should treat one another with respect.*

7. **God's *Name*** – *The name of God should be revered and used only with respect.*

8. **Golden Mean** - *The desirable middle between two extremes: one extreme of excess and the other of deficiency. For example, courage is a virtue, but in excess could be recklessness, and if inadequate could be cowardice.*

D. Killers, Liars, and Thieves - *Unfortunately, not all human beings are decent people who adhere to the standards listed above. You must be alert to the fact that there are killers, liars, thieves, sexual predators and all manner of other dishonorable human beings and criminals who will take advantage of you and your family given the opportunity to do so.*

E. The Decent and the Indecent - *It has been said that there are only two races of mankind: the decent and the indecent.[3]*

- *Both races are everywhere in all groups of society.*

- *Most indecent people don't consider themselves to be indecent or acknowledge or advertise their vices. They may seem like model citizens until you get to know them well.*

- *All human beings have their own less serious vices that affect their inter-personal relationships with family, friends and co-workers.*

F. The Challenges - *Three challenges of human life are to:*

1. *Maximize your virtues*
2. *Minimize your vices*
3. *Learn to honor God and encourage one another*

According to Award winning actor Audrey Hepburn, makeup can only make you look pretty on the outside. Unfortunately, it can't help if you are ugly on the inside, that is, unless maybe you eat the makeup.[4]

IV. Human Rights and Responsibilities

A. Rights

There are basic rights and fundamental freedoms to which each human being is entitled. These rights proceed from natural law as a birthright endowed by our creator equally to all human beings.

Just democratic societies usually recognize these rights, although enforcement varies from country to country. Widely recognized human rights generally fall into the following seven categories: [5]

1. ***Personal Security Rights:*** *including the right to life, freedom from slavery, the right of self-defense, and other rights against crimes such as murder, massacres, torture, rape and assault.*

2. ***Rights of Freedom and Liberty:*** *freedom of religion, freedom of association, the right of assembly, right to bear arms and freedom of movement within national borders.*

3. ***Political Freedoms:*** *guarantee participation in the political process through freedom of expression, the right to vote, the right of peaceful protest and other means of participation in the political process.*

4. ***Rights of Due Legal Process:*** *hold all citizens to be innocent until proven guilty and require a fair, speedy and public trial. They provide protection against abuses of the legal system such as imprisonment without trial, secret trials, self-incrimination, cruel and unusual punishment or retroactive application of new laws. These rights also prevent unreasonable searches and seizures of people's property.*

5. **Rights of Equality:** *guarantee equal treatment in the legal process, equal citizenship and protection against various types of discrimination.*

6. **Economic and Welfare Rights:** *establish rights to own property and enforce contracts. Also, entitlement to minimum wages and other minimum working conditions; indigent medical care; rights to education, and protection against severe poverty and starvation.*

7. **Group Rights:** *include only special rights for protection against ethnic genocide. These are the same personal security rights that apply to everyone. There is never justification for giving special economic or political rights to some groups over others.*

B. Responsibilities

To **deserve** and enjoy **the rights** of a citizen in a civilized society, you must **accept** the **responsibilities and duties** of a citizen. People live and cooperate in societies to enjoy the **mutual benefits** of **civilization** without which life could be poor, nasty, brutish and short.[6]

Duty - Civil cooperation requires that you accept certain duties and responsibilities including prohibitions on offending those with whom you must live.

We have a duty to make sure the effects we have on other people are beneficial.

The significant duties and responsibilities of a modern human being are generally prioritized in order of faith, family and society and they include the following:

1) **If you** are of **faith**, you have a spiritual duty to honor God and the requirements of your faith.

2) You have a moral **duty to work hard** to develop virtue and overcome selfishness.

   - Part of the meaning of life is found in unselfishly carrying out our roles and responsibilities to other people as part of our duties to the society in which we live.

- *This gives us the responsibility to lead a **socially** and **morally meaningful** life.*

3) *Your life should be a quest to **improve the character** of your soul and the soul of your community.*

- *Like the knights of old, you have the responsibility to discipline yourself to avoid gluttony, drunkenness, drug abuse and the other addictions that want to help you destroy yourself.*

- *You must protect your health so you can contribute **back to** society more than you **take from** society.*

- *Become a strong, capable giver, not a weak selfish taker.*

4) *If you have a **family**:*

- *You have a duty to raise, discipline and nurture your children properly.*

- *You have a duty to honor and protect your spouse and family.*

- *You have a duty to make the very best effort possible to provide for yourself and your family before expecting help from others.*

5) *You have an obligation to **honor your parents** and to take care of them in their old age even as they have taken care of you in your childhood.*

6) *You should earn the respect of others by being very good at your job or profession.*

- *You have a duty to **contribute to the common** good by seeking wisdom and understanding in all things.*

- *Be careful not to think yourself so smart as to be beyond correction, instruction or improvement.*

7) *By way of contribution to the common good of your society, you have a duty to refrain from polluting the moral environment with consistent expression of pessimism and negativity that brings others low in the attitude of mind and spirit.*

- *Avoid foul, coarse, vile language (cursing, etc.) and the antagonistic discourse of strife that cheapens and weakens your spiritual power.*

- *Communicate in language that elevates the soul of all who read or hear it, thereby contributing to the well-being of your friends, neighbors and fellow citizens.*

- *If you are in a bad mood, you have a duty to behave as if you're not, by having the moral courage to face down your negativity rather than spreading it about like a disease.*

- *You have a duty to overcome the ever-present temptation to criticize and be negative by keeping your attitude and communication positive in all matters.*

- *Where there are problems, think and talk about the solutions you can work towards instead of thinking and talking about the problems and the difficulties.*

8) *We have a duty to inspire one another and especially the young with the moral example of a positive, virtuous and noble life well lived. Encourage more and criticize less!*

- *These things are much, much more important, challenging and difficult than they may seem.*

- *You owe your fellow human beings your very best effort, strength and courage to develop the virtues necessary to become part of the solution to your society's troubles.*

- *Do not allow yourself to fall into the bad habits that would make you just another weak part of your society's problems.*

- *Until you are spiritually strong enough to help them, do not associate with negative, immoral people.*

  o *Avoid negative folks lest their harmful energy infect your attitude and pull you down the slippery slope into their selfish, undisciplined state of spiritual weakness and decay, where their misery always desires company.*

     o   *Make extra sure you are not one of them.*

9) *You have an obligation to obey the just laws of your society, to seek justice instead of revenge, and you have a responsibility to pay the lawful taxes that are necessary to make your community and your country strong.*

   If you do not like the society in which you live, either leave and go to another country, or work through the political process to inspire change in a peaceful and positive manner.

10) *You should respect the dignity of other human beings and help those who are in legitimate need of encouragement or support.*

   - *Practice mercy and truth, and do not gossip or put down others in a vain attempt to make yourself look cool.*

   - *In an age of cynical criticism, we should be a much-needed voice of encouragement to the other people in our lives.*

11) *If you live in a democracy, you have the responsibility to become informed about the issues of your time and to participate in your self -government by voting or even running for political office.*

   - *Just because you feel passionately about something does not make your view correct.*

   - *You have a duty to study all sides of issues and problems about which you are concerned from an unbiased point of view.*

   - *This serious obligation to the principles of truth and wisdom is necessary, lest you do more harm to your society than good.*

12) *You should defend your country when necessary, and you should support those, who by doing so, are put in harm's way.*

13) *We have an important moral and social obligation to restrain physical sickness and disease.*

   - *We are obliged, therefore, to use fully proven vaccinations, medications, good hygiene and other preventive measures to avoid catching and spreading illness and infection.*

- *An effective means of avoiding colds, flu and some other sicknesses is to scrub your hands thoroughly for at least 21 seconds after being in public or coming into contact with an ill person. Shake hands less and use fist bumps more.*

14) *You have an obligation to educate yourself to become an economically productive individual who produces as much or more than you consume. If you take more from society than you give, you become an economic parasite.*

- *You have a duty not to waste economic resources, but to use them wisely on your job.*

- *You also have a duty to become a selective consumer who compares price, quality and overall value before purchasing goods and services.*

- *You should volunteer some of your spare time to local schools, libraries and other helping agencies.*

- *You have a duty to safeguard the environment by minimizing pollution and ecological destruction.*

According to Father Theodore Hesberg, President Emeritus of Notre Dame University

- *Compassion is **concern** that someone should do something about a situation.*

- *Competency is having the **ability** to do it.*

- *Commitment is the **willingness** to do it yourself.*

"...each individual has duties to other individuals and to the community to which they belong..."
...From the Preamble of the International Covenant on Civil and Political Rights

V. Human Courtesy and Good Manners

Human societies have developed informal systems or guidelines for interpersonal behavior known as good manners or courtesy.

- *These systems are designed to reduce strife and friction between citizens as they live and interact with one another on a daily basis.*

- *Like traffic rules, they promote a smoother, more orderly flow of human activity with less stress and conflict.*

With billions of people on the planet interacting constantly with one another in an increasingly global society, it is important to keep the personal interaction as pleasant, fair and orderly as possible.

- *Success is much more likely to occur for those who have mastered the art of courtesy and the practice of good manners.*

- *Courtesy and good manners are based on unselfish concern for the feelings and well-being of others.*

- *They generally embody the principle of **acting toward other people the way you would like them to act toward you**.*

- *The system of kind and gracious behavior toward others works best to the extent that it is understood and practiced by all.*

"Encourage one another and build one another up"
...1ˢᵗ Thessalonians 5:11

It is especially important for spouses to treat one another with good manners and courteous behavior in order to preserve mutual respect in the marriage and to model kind and gracious behavior for their children.

The specific expressions of good manners and courtesy are a learned behavior usually taught to children by their parents, and they vary somewhat among human cultures.

*The following 27 common expressions of **courtesy and good manners** are found in most human societies:*

1. *Always preface a request with "Please" as in "please hand me the book."*

2. *Always say "Thank you" when someone does anything for you, be it great or small.*

3. *Apologize and say you are sorry when you are wrong or if you inconvenience or falsely accuse another. People know it takes courage to admit you are wrong, and they respect those who do.*

4. *Maintain normal eye contact while in conversation with others, but do not stare at them.*

5. *Do not interrupt others when they are speaking. This is a very common problem.*

6. *Do not cut in line when people are lined up and waiting.*

7. *Do not put other people down and don't make harmful fun or jokes about them or their misfortune.*

8. *Avoid talking too loudly in conversation.*

9. *Spend more time listening than talking.*

10. *Cover your mouth when yawning.*

11. *Avoid complaining and negative talk; find something positive to say or say nothing at all.*

12. *Be encouraging in conversation with others and help lift their spirits.*

13. *Don't brag on yourself or try to impress others; it only makes you look insecure.*

14. *Be quick to praise others and slow to criticize them.*

15. *Treat other people with respect by being gracious and helpful instead of rude and selfish.*

16. *Don't chew food with your mouth open.*

17. *Don't call people derogatory names.*

18. *Avoid cursing, swearing and the use of other crude or vulgar language.*

19. *Pass gas and ill-informed opinions quietly when in the presence of others.*

20. *Dress somewhat modestly in public.*

21. *Avoid burping or belching in the company of others and apologize if you do so.*

22. *Be considerate of other people and keep the volume down when watching television, playing music etc.*

23. *When calling on the telephone, identify yourself and the person you wish to speak with in somewhat the following manner: "This is John Smith calling for Mary Jones." Do not expect people to recognize your voice.*

24. *Send thank you messages or otherwise acknowledge your thanks and appreciation to those who help you or give you gifts.*

25. *Avoid gossip and speak ill of no one behind his or her back.*

26. *In all things big and small, be considerate of other people and look for ways to help them.*

27. *Spell and grammar check your emails and written correspondence for they are part of the image others hold of you.*

"Manners are rules of unselfishness"
...Jennie Bishop[7]

Similar pointers put another way:[8]

1. *Keep chains on your tongue; always say less than you think. Cultivate a pleasant, persuasive voice. **How you say it** often counts more than what you say.*

2. *Make promises sparingly and keep them faithfully.*

3. *Never let an opportunity pass, to say a kind word to somebody. Praise good work, regardless of who does it. If correction is needed, criticize helpfully, never in a destructive manner.*

4. *Be genuinely interested in others. Let everyone you meet feel that you regard him or her as a person of importance.*

5. *Be cheerful. Keep the corners of your mouth turned up. Hide your pains, worries and disappointments under a smile.*

6. *Keep an open mind on all controversial questions. Discuss without arguing. It is possible to disagree and yet be friendly.*

7. *Never, engage in gossip. Make it a rule to say nothing about another unless it is something good.*

8. *Be careful of other people's feelings. A laugh at another's expense is rarely worth the effort, and it may hurt where least expected.*

9. *Pay no attention to cutting remarks that others may make about you. Learn to live above such comments.*

10. *Don't be too anxious about your rights and having favors repaid. Let the satisfaction of helping others serve as its own reward.*

Courtesy and good manners are a sign of a considerate and usually well-educated individual who can get along and work well with other people. These people are generally preferred by employers and are often promoted. The higher one goes in an organization, the more stressful the work, making it all the more important that leaders and managers know how to work under pressure without unduly aggravating one another.

Knowledge and practice of good manners can be a great boost to life in general while requiring very little effort to master. If you want your children to succeed in the game of life, teach them the rules of the game.

VI. Summary

Discussed in this chapter were the following articles of good citizenship:

Social Contract - The vital social contract that makes a democracy work is the agreement that we will all be governed equally according to laws agreed to by the majority of our elected representatives.

Illegal Conduct – Behavior considered so detrimental to society that it is prohibited by law.

Immoral Conduct – Behavior violating a society's concept of good and decent (moral) activity.

Other Standards of Conduct – Other behavior considered unacceptable in most societies.

Rights - Basic rights and fundamental freedoms to which each human being is entitled.

Responsibilities - To deserve a citizen's rights, you must accept a citizen's duties.

Manners - Guidelines for smooth interpersonal behavior are known as good manners or courtesy.

Not long after the economic development dinner at Brenda and Carolyn's house, Brenda told Carter that Mr. Cannon would like to see him the next day at 10:00 in the morning about potential employment. She helped him pick out the most appropriate of her late husband's clothes and coached him on the best ways to handle job interviews.

Carter felt confident because his parents were both working professionals who raised him with the best of manners and a positive professional attitude.

Chapter 1 Soul of a Good Citizen

The following is a famous **short course in human relations,** the original source of which is unknown:

The most important words in the human language

"I admit I made a mistake"

The five most important words:

"You did a good job."

The four most important words:

"What is your opinion?"

The three most important words:

"If you please"

The two most important words:

"Thank you"

The single most important word:

"We"

The least important word:

"I"

"Great minds discuss ideas, average minds discuss events, small minds discuss other people."
...Admiral Hyman Rickover USN

"...recognition of the inherent dignity and of the equal and inalienable rights of all members of the human family is the foundation of freedom, justice and peace in the world."
...Preamble to the United Nations
Universal Declaration of Human Rights

It is said that an Eastern monarch once charged his wise men to invent for him a statement to be ever in view, and which should be true and appropriate in all times and all situations. After months of thought, they presented him with the words:
And this too shall pass.[9]

---

[1] JosephsonInstitute.org

[2] Marchette Chute, *The Search for God*, Robert Sumner Publishing, 1969, p.164

[3] Victor E. Frankl, *Man's Search for Meaning*, Beacon Press, Boston, p.86

[4] Reader's Digest, October 2016, p.83

[5] Online encyclopedia on Human Rights, p2 of 9

[6] Thomas Hobbes, *The Leviathan*

[7] Jennie Bishop, *I Want to Teach my Child about Manners*, Standard Publishing, p.9

[8] From the Arlington bulletin via Church of Christ Newsletter, Saffron St. Christchurch, 1988 and Sycamore Chapel bulletin, Apr. 17, 1996, p. 2

[9] Roy P. Basler *The Collected Works of Abraham Lincoln*, Volume III, "Address Before the Wisconsin State Agricultural Society, Milwaukee, Wisconsin" (September 30, 1859), pp. 481-482.

Chapter 2
Laws of the Soul

C arter goes to see Mr. Cannon, and is directed to an attractive house where he is led into a well-appointed office. Mr. Cannon arrives shortly, a lean and fit older man with gray hair and intelligent eyes. They greet one another again.

"I understand," begins Mr. Cannon, "that you are a scholar and a spiritual pilgrim, but that you seek now to learn the art of making money. What marketable talent or experience do you have? What is it that you've learned, and what are you able to do?"

"My college degree is in economics; I can think quickly, read and write well, analyze thoroughly and communicate effectively, and finally, I can wait patiently," replies Carter.

"Ok, great. Please wait here for a moment," says Mr. Cannon.

He leaves the room and returns with some papers, asking, "Can you read this?"

Carter looks at the paper on which a legal contract has been written and begins to read its contents aloud.

"Excellent," says Mr. Cannon. "And would you please explain the contract and write an analysis of its benefits and its drawbacks as they would apply to each party to the proposed contract?"

Soul meets soul on lover's lips.
...Poet P.B. Shelley

Human Spiritual Powers

Mr. Cannon hands him a piece of paper and a pen, and Carter thinks and writes for a few minutes and returns the paper.

"Your analysis and your writing are excellent," the businessman says. "Although, we need to get to know one another and discuss many other things, I invite you to be my guest and to live here for a while."

Carter thanks him and accepts the good businessman's kind offer. Carter still eats only once a day, eating neither meat nor drinking alcoholic beverages.

Mr. Cannon tells him about the business, shows him the merchandise and storage-rooms and explains the accounts and how they are set up. Carter learns many new things; he listens a lot and speaks little. The partners conduct their business with care and often with passion, and he tries hard to learn from them all that he can.

Carter asks the partners if they know of APOLLYON and they say they are aware that the organization is stirring up discontent and trying to push Socialism on the country. Carter tells them of his involvement against APOLLYON in case they would rather he leave because of it.

They advise Carter that like most taxpayers, they are against APOLLYON and what they stand for. They add that Carter is more welcome than before, and that if there is trouble, they will be with him.

Mr. Cannon says, "There comes a time when good people have to stand up together against tyranny."

"I would add," says Mr. Bell, "that APOLLYON with their tactics of violence and Socialism amount to tyranny pure and simple. All they want is to end up with the political power to run this country into the ground while they get rich in the process."

Carter is not in Mr. Cannon's house for long, before he begins taking part in his landlord's business. The businessmen gradually pass duties of writing important letters and contracts on to him and they get into the habit of discussing most important affairs with him.

"You don't have a soul. You are a soul. You have a body."
...Professor and author C.S. Lewis

Chapter 2 Laws of the Soul

They soon see that Carter knows little about rice and corn, shipping and trade, but that he acts in a professional manner. He is calm and patient and customers like doing business with him because he listens well and understands their needs.

"This young man," Mr. Cannon says to his partner, "has a mysterious quality of effortless success about him. I can't tell if it's due to a lucky combination of talent and effort or what; but my only concern is that he seems unconcerned about failure or loss."

Mr. Bell said, "Why not make him a minority partner and see if he responds differently with a small share in the business?"

Mr. Cannon follows his partner's advice, and as a partner, Carter seems to find more pleasure in his work. However, Carter still accepts losses when they occur with patience, but he always learns from his mistakes.

On one occasion, Carter travels to the Middle East to explore the possibility of importing dates. While there, he decides to visit the historic section of Jerusalem to do a little sightseeing.

The ancient, sunbaked, walled city of David is rich in the traditions of three world religions, Judaism, Christianity and Islam, and it plays an important role in the history of all three.

While touring Jerusalem, he visits the Temple Mount. There he meets a slim, dark haired teenager selling souvenirs. The earnest young man says he is a student working his way through his last year of high school.

Carter, having never been out of his own country, is fascinated by the diverse culture of the area and takes an interest in the young man whose name is Joseph Wright. Joseph speaks very good English and offers to act as a guide and translator for Carter.

For three days, Joseph helps Carter with date vendors all around the great city, and in the process, they become friends. Carter learns that Joseph is from a poor family, and he is struggling to pay for school.

One evening, Joseph graciously invites Carter to his parent's home for dinner. Carter gladly agrees, for he has seen enough of the city's tourist sites, and he is by now more interested in seeing how the local people live.

Joseph's mother Mira is a small round woman with the worries of poverty etched deep in the lines of her olive complexion, and her dark hair is laced with streaks of gray. His thin, bearded father Ahmed is an invalid in his fifties injured some years ago in a construction accident where he had been a stone mason.

The Jewish family has three children of which Joseph is the oldest. His parents are interested in Carter as he is the first foreigner, they have met. They pepper him with questions with Joseph translating for them.

After dinner, he enjoys more translated conversation with his hosts who inquire to a considerable degree about Carter's concept of good human character and trustworthiness.

Eventually, with the evening growing late, Carter expresses his genuine appreciation for the dinner and the opportunity to spend time with Joseph's family. Joseph asks if Carter might have one more day to see something of great personal importance to which Carter agrees before returning to his hotel.

The next day Joseph arrives at the hotel and asks Carter to his house for lunch, saying his father wants to show him something he has kept hidden for 30 years.

Carter is intrigued and readily agrees, but only if they let him bring lunch. Consequently, Joseph and Carter spend the morning shopping in open-air food markets where the locals shop for food.

After lunch, Joseph's father brings out a beat up, old, leather-wrapped manuscript. He says he found it one-night years ago while sifting through piles of discarded rubble from an underground excavation site near the Western Wall of the Temple Mount. He says the 16-page manuscript was enclosed in the remains of an old leather-bound wine container.

"The function of socialism is to raise suffering to a higher level."
...Author and Journalist Norman Mailer

Chapter 2 Laws of the Soul

Neither his father nor Joseph could read the document because it was written in a strange language. Joseph's father felt it was valuable, but he was reluctant to show it to anyone locally because he was sure it would be taken from him, and that he would be cheated out of any money it might be worth.

Joseph had made a copy by hand that he was hoping to get translated, except that he feared it would require that he explain where he got it. Otherwise, he was going to try to get his copy duplicated on a replicator to sell to tourists. That too had some risk that it could be traced back to him if it turned out to have value.

Carter suggests he take Joseph's hand written copy back to his hotel to have a copy made on the hotel replicator. He could give back the handwritten copy to Joseph, and take the other copy back to the states to see if he could find a way to get it translated, which he would do in strict confidence.

"It could be just a very old list of business transactions, ledgers or a record of some other mundane activity of little historical value," says Carter. "On the other hand, it might contain invaluable wisdom from a forgotten time, and the original could be worth a great deal of money."

In any case, Carter says he will let them know by mail as soon as he finds out something. It is agreeable to them, and Carter finds it on his mind a lot as he returns home.

Upon his return, Carter tells his partners that the trip has been a success as he found several suppliers of wholesome dates with whom they could contract for a favorable price.

Later, Carter does some research into Middle Eastern language experts and finds a Professor Crozier in a neighboring state who agrees to look at the manuscript. The professor is an older man who lived in the Middle East for years, and he speaks several Middle Eastern languages.

A couple of days later, Carter goes to see Professor Crozier. The heavy set, professor with thick grey hair and wire-rimmed glasses concludes that the ancient document was written in an obscure, early Middle Eastern script that had not been in use for several thousand years since the time of King Solomon. He adds, however, that there are other known languages through which they can cross translate it into English.

The professor's office is paneled in rich Mediterranean wood with shelves full of old books and artifacts. The professor places the manuscript is on a modern light table with a large magnifier. After a while, Professor Crozier says, "The document seems to be divided into three sections." In addition, he asks where the original document was found. Carter explains the situation in general terms keeping names to himself.

The professor says he is aware of an incident many years ago that might shed some light on the subject. A chamber off a tunnel under the temple mount had been excavated secretly by two religious scholars who later claimed to have seen the Ark of the Covenant there.

The covert excavation was discovered soon after it began, resulting in a massive brawl between young Jews and Arabs in the area.

To keep a fragile peace between religions, the tunnel was quickly sealed with concrete by security forces. The sealed entrance can be seen still from the Western Wall Tunnel.

The secret night excavation and the brawl might explain why the old manuscript had been overlooked in the rubble from the tunnel, thought Carter.

With Carter helping, they soon piece together the title that reads "Laws and Principles of Human Spiritual Power."

This greatly intrigues both Carter and the Professor who decide they should get together on weekends to work on the rest of the document. Carter enjoys working with the jolly, rotund Professor; nevertheless, Carter always keeps the manuscript with him.

Carter sends a letter to Joseph Wright bringing them up to date on the status of the manuscript. He tells them he will continue to work on the translation unless they notify him to do otherwise.

Two weeks later, he receives a reply stating simply "Please continue." In the meantime, Carter and the Professor have completed work on the first section entitled **Laws of the Human Soul.**

Their translation is presented on the following pages:

Handbook of the Soul
Laws of the Soul

I. Preview

*Set forth herein are Ten **evident laws** concerning development of the human soul, knowledge of which will help our people as their souls move through challenges and difficulty along their earthly journeys.*

***1**. **Soul's Development** - The purpose of our lives is to pursue the advancement of our souls.*

***2**. **Soul's Maturity** - Spiritually disciplined choices mature your spirit and soul.*

***3. Transforming Effect** - The goals of **wisdom, truth** and **virtue** must be forged into our human character through **honorable** living.*

***4. Action – Reaction** - What happens to you matters not nearly so much as your reaction to it.*

***5. Depth vs. Length** - Human life is to be valued for its depth not its length.*

***6. Tools of Development** - Temptations, problems and successes develop your soul.*

***7. Treatment of Others** - Spiritual character is cultivated by treatment of other people.*

***8. Focus of Development** - Your body is tailored to the developmental requirements of your soul.*

9. Life is Not Fair - Each soul is challenged in ways unique to its own development.

10. Law of Change – If you want to get to a place or condition where you are not, you must be willing to change from where or what you are.

II. Introduction

One of the great mysteries of human existence concerns the interior dynamics of the human soul and the principles involved in its **earthly operation**.

Understanding the plain truths and simple principles in this document should be easy, but putting them into **practice regularly** seems to be the most difficult and decisive challenge facing every human soul.

All our human functions, faculties and powers are good, and to direct them rightly is wisdom, holiness and happiness; to direct them wrongly is folly, madness and possibly evil resulting by degree in the soul's corruption.

Divinity has established physical laws such as the law of gravity that govern the operation of everything in the cosmos. Like the physical laws, Divinity has spiritual laws governing the activity and growth of the human soul.

Where there is wrong, it comes from the fear or selfishness of human beings whose focus is so completely upon themselves that they distort the application of these spiritual laws and principles creating immorality and evil as they do so.

The spiritual progress of our souls depends upon our right choices and actions not upon our knowledge and understanding. Therefore, we must put into choices the knowledge and understanding we gain or it does not transform us.

For example, understanding how birds fly and flying are two very different things.

"Life is a grindstone. Whether it grinds you down or polishes you up depends on what you are made of." [1]

Likewise, understanding the meaning of forgiveness and forgiving someone are two very different things. As wise men have noted, "Well done is much better than well said!"

If we are to make spiritual progress in this life, we must be doing something of practical benefit for our people and actually living God's spiritual laws and principles in the process.

Carter remarks to the professor that even in antiquity they recognized the importance of walking the walk instead of just talking the talk.

III. The Nature of the Soul's Development

*The first section of the ancient script went on to say that, the following **ten laws** are related to the **nature of the soul's development**. Some items are similar, but restated for clarity with a slightly different perspective.*

1. Soul's Development: *The purpose of our lives is to promote our soul's advancement not our physical comfort. Spiritual maturity is the work of a lifetime that involves many, many steps. The meaning of your human life is in the opportunity it provides to develop, align, balance and refine the temperament of your eternal soul and the spiritual character at its core.*

- ***Decisions You Make*** *- Part of the improvement in your immortal soul and spiritual character will come about through the decisions you make and the ways in which you cope with the big and small challenges human experience brings you.*

- ***Self-Imposed Difficulties*** *- Self-evident spiritual powers are used by the wiser among us to help them avoid self-imposed difficulties as they journey through this life. All can learn to do this.*

- ***Positive Coping*** *- Learning to cope well with adversity, success, failure and one another on the basis of positive rather than negative principles is part of the process of spiritual growth.*

- ***Way We Act*** *- Thus, in the long run, what physically happens to us is not important; what really matters is the way in which we choose to act and respond to the people and events in our lives.*

- *Gracious Spiritual Strength* - *An important spiritual objective is to develop the life force in our souls toward a balanced level of gracious strength that is complete and devoid of negative and selfish motivation.*

2. Soul Maturity - *The maturity of your spirit and soul are enhanced whenever you learn to manage the challenges, temptations and opportunities of life by making more* **positive** *and* **spiritually disciplined choices**.

- *This is part of the* **eternal purifying process** *of spiritual transformation and closer alignment with the Divine mystery of God.*

- *The basis of all creation is evidently spiritual.*

- *The higher dimensions of existence, i.e., heaven, must be more spiritual in nature and may require a much higher degree of universal spiritual harmony.*

Higher Dimensions - *In order to progress in the higher dimensions of existence, we must be of spiritually stronger character meaning more resistant to selfishness, temptation, fear and negativity.*

We must be more capable of maintaining a positive and gracious spiritual temperament, which should be reflected, in our human character and disposition.

The meaning of our earthly existence is in the opportunity it provides:

- *To* **grow** *and* **strengthen** *the* **positive, virtuous power** *of our spirits and souls*

- *To purge or* **reform** *our* **selfish, fearful, negative** *and* **corrupt character traits**

- *Part of life's purpose is to understand and develop the power of our spirit; power that is vital to our mental and physical well-being.*

- *Abusing this power depletes our spirits and siphons some of the life force itself from our physical bodies.*[2]

3. _Transforming Effect_ - **_Wisdom, truth_** and **_virtue_** _must be forged into our human character through_ **_honorable_** _living._

- _The transformation of your soul must be accomplished with action, by making daily choices and living the consequences of those choices._

- _We must learn through experience how to control and reform the negative aspects of our character._

- _The process of spiritual growth occurs as we increase our ability to cope more positively with our physical, mental and emotional challenges._

- _It has been said that humans often feel overwhelmed when they realize the amount of wrong thinking to which they are addicted._[3]

- _We try to cast out selfish negative thoughts, but they will come right back. However, little by little, freedom and deliverance does come through continued effort._

- _We must shift the focus of our being from ourselves to Godliness and the needs of other people._

Condition of Mind - _Self is not an entity that has to be cast out, but a condition of mind to be enlightened and changed._

Challenging Environment - _Spiritual development must necessarily take place in a challenging environment of opportunity, difficulty and temptation, as is the environment on Earth._

The imperfect, often unfair condition of human society on earth is where, for example, transgression by one person can be used to teach forgiveness to another.

With your thoughts, you are the creator of what your life becomes, not just its manager.
...Unknown

4. _Action – Response or Reaction_: _As previously stated, that which happens to us matters not nearly so much as our response or reaction to it. We always have a choice to respond positively or react negatively to the circumstances and events in our lives._

The essence of human development is in learning to **manage** spiritually our response to all positive or negative circumstances and situations by disciplining our thoughts.

- **_Accelerated Progress_** _- Our spiritual progress can be sped-up with a conscious and continuous effort to improve our character._

- **_Recognize_** _- We must recognize the aspects of our temperament and character that need improvement and change our thought and behavior accordingly._

- **_Changed Habits_** _- Changed thinking leads to changed behavior, which, in as little as 30 days, can lead to changed habits, which lead over time to changed character._

- **_Little Consequence_** _- The things and events that physically and materially affect us over the course of our lives are of little consequence. This is especially so when compared to the spiritual importance of learning to respond courageously, positively and graciously to whatever happens in the daily challenges and opportunities along our human journeys._

5. _Depth vs. Length_: _Human life is a journey to be valued for its **depth** and **purpose** not necessarily for the length of time over which your life extends._

- _The depth of your experience relates to the obstacles you overcome and the people you help. Purpose refers to the purpose to which you devote your life._

- _These obstacles and the people you help are your opportunities for the development of your soul._

- _The difference between your spirit when it comes into the earth as a human fetus and your same spirit that will leave your body at death is the change in your eternal character that resulted_ *from the lessons of living human life over the period of your earthly existence.*

- *The goal of your human existence is **not** simply to stay alive for as long as possible but to gain the spiritual wisdom and discipline necessary for the transformation of your soul. It has been said that the proper measure of a life is not its **duration** but its **donation** and **maturation**.*

"This stuff seems pretty clear and relevant," said Professor Crozier, "although it involves a complete change in perspective on life. It does make more sense than most of the other explanations for human existence that I've heard."

"Yeah, me too," agreed Carter.

6. _Tools of Development_: *The problems, trials, pain, successes, failures, pleasure, stress and temptations of human existence cannot be avoided. They affect all human beings, in varying degree, regardless of wealth, status or circumstance.*

*Life's experiences are among the **tools of human character development** through which your soul may grow and mature.*

Your Chiseled Soul - *Your responses to the challenges and opportunities of life are chiseling the character of your soul. It has been said that adversity can be a bridge to a deeper relationship with God.[4]*

- *Challenges and opportunities are not designed to frustrate or punish you. They are simply the tools and apparatus of the human stage of spiritual development; much as a human baby's physical development involves falling down repeatedly in the process of learning to walk.*

- *One of the great secrets of your soul is that through your thought process your soul can attract what you love and desire or that which you fear and mistrust.*

> **"You can transform everything around you**
> **if you will transform yourself."**
> *...Philosopher James Allen*

- *It depends, largely, on the kind of thoughts you allow in your mind, for you can learn through both suffering and success.*

- *Spiritual development is a gradual, purifying and eternal process.*

- *Several times each day, we are given opportunities to react negatively or respond positively to small frustrations, vexing situations and temptations to lose our temper or lose our serenity.*

- *These situations and temptations should be recognized as opportunities to make progress by improving our behavior and making better choices.*

- *Spiritual character is developed by the moral and ethical choices we make, with "temptation's attractions" often present as one of the choices.*

- **As You Choose - So Shall You Be** - *Each moral choice should be handled a little better than the last "for as you choose, so shall you be."*
  - *When we are under pressure and tempted to be angry, we must choose to be patient.*
  - *When tempted to be deceitful, we must choose to be honest.*
  - *Integrity is developed by overcoming the temptation to be dishonest at all levels of life from petty situations to critical decisions.*
  - *Each time you choose, ask yourself if it's the choice the person **you want to be** would make. For as you choose, so will you become.*

7. Treatment of Other People - *Sometimes our spiritual integrity is challenged on a large scale, in situations where there appears to be a great deal at stake.*

- *The real issue, however, is always the cultivation of our soul's spiritual character and how well we respond to the pressure and temptation of the moment and especially how well we treat other people and, or animals in the process.*

- *Over the course of your lifetime, thousands upon thousands of opportunities will occur to handle people or situations in more gracious, more positive, more generous or more unselfish ways.*

- *The extent to which you do so is a measure of your progress as a human soul.*

- *Evangelist Billy Graham said God gave us two hands: one with which to receive and the other with which to give.*

Negative Frustrating People - *The most difficult, negative and frustrating people in life may be here because their spiritual characters are immature or well out of balance.*

However, their presence can cause others to develop the positive spiritual coping mechanisms necessary for dealing with negativity, dishonesty and adversity.

- *Each relationship we develop can serve to help us become more conscious and disciplined about the way we relate to one another. Judging other people and being critical of them serves no useful purpose.*

- *Each time we interface with difficult people we are being given the opportunity to rise above their petty, insecure, argumentative or controlling ways. The less they "get to" us by creating a negative response in us, the more mature in character we become.*

- *Some relationships are necessarily painful because they involve learning unpleasant things about ourselves and facing our limitations, which are not things we tend to do with enthusiasm.*

*8. **Focus of Development**: The particular physical and mental attributes of your human body are tailored to the developmental requirements of your soul; and our families of origin may be divinely assigned to help us learn some of the lessons we need to learn in this lifetime such as courage or the ability to forgive etc.*

- *Therefore, you may be born, by design, into a specific family with a genetic propensity for certain problems i.e., alcoholism, allergies, strong or poor health, special talent or any particular combination of physical abilities and deficiencies.*

- *Everyone in your life plays a role in your development, and unfortunately, some relationships are necessarily painful in that regard.*

- *Your abilities and deficiencies are of such a nature that, over a lifetime, they will focus and challenge your soul's character development into those areas where it most needs improvement, such as patience, self-control, faith, humility or unselfishness or any other virtues.*

- *Spiritual growth is not assured and neither is the course of your life.*

- *So, while the course of human life is not predestined, many of the physical attributes, traits and other characteristics you are born with may be tailored to ensure that your soul is exposed to the kinds of challenges and opportunities it requires for its particular growth and development.*

The direction of your life and the development of your spirit and soul depend upon:

- *The kind of thoughts you permit in your mind*

- *The choices you make and actions you take*

- *The courage, will and effort you apply toward character improvement*

- *The recognition that you alone are responsible for the quality of the being you're becoming*

**"Desire little
Put others first
Embrace simplicity"**
...Tao Te Ching (The way of life) Lao Tzu

*When faced with the challenges and difficulties of life, don't just **go** through them, **grow** through them. Doing so best takes a victor's attitude and an understanding that some of these challenges are painful character-building trials and tests.* [5]

9. Life is Not Fair: *Human life on earth may seem to be unfair because it appears to be much more difficult for some than for others. However, each human soul is challenged in ways that are unique to its own development, so each human journey is different.*

In addition, human beings are at different levels of development, so they can handle different levels of opportunity, difficulty and success.

- *Human beings also bring about many of their own problems because they are free to act and respond to their own circumstances and to make their own choices in life.*

- *More difficulty is often the result of negative responses and **poor choices**, while less difficulty can be the result of positive responses and better choices.*

- *The journeys of human life are not designed to be fair in the sense that you would have no more difficulty or success in life than another would have.*

- *Self-pity, griping, complaining and adopting the victim ethic are self-defeating modes of human behavior. The "victim ethic" is a false belief that your lack of success in life is due to the actions of others that are somehow holding you down.*

- *You must work hard to develop the positive spiritual skills necessary to cope with your own challenges, even if your worldly circumstance and problems seem out of proportion to those of others.*

- *Ironically, this is often best achieved by shifting focus from your own problems to actively helping other people deal with their problems.*

It can be helpful to realize that life just is not supposed to be fair, and that **we are all suffering, in part, from the consequences of our own choices**.

Try to remember that the seemingly unfair aspects of your life, along with everything else you experience are being used to shape the character of your immortal soul.

Therefore, it is best not to harbor bitterness or resentment but to handle your challenges with courage and honor and to do what is right by other people in the process.

10. <u>Law of Change</u> – If you want to get to a place or condition where you are not, you must be willing to change from where or what you are. This is both a physical and spiritual law.

Human beings don't always embrace change especially as they mature, however, to be alive is to change physically as we grow and age. The very meaning of life is the change our souls undergo while in this dimension.

We need not fear change as long as we are guiding the change to the improvement of our spiritual character and the qualities of our soul that will lead ultimately from our present condition to an infinitely better one.

IV. Summary

The following laws were reviewed in this section:

1. Spiritual Development - The purpose of our lives is the spiritual advancement of our souls.

2. Soul Maturity - Spiritually disciplined choices mature your soul.

3. Transforming Effect - The goals of **wisdom, truth** and **virtue** must be forged into our human character through **honorable** living.

4. Action – Reaction - What happens to us matters not nearly so much as our response to it.

5. Depth vs. Length - Human life is to be valued not for its length, but for the extent to which it transforms your soul.

6. Tools of Development - *Temptations, problems and successes develop your soul, so do not just **go** through them, **grow** through them.*

7. Treatment of Others - *Spiritual character is developed in part through the way we treat other people.*

8. Focus of Development - *Your body's strengths and weaknesses are tailored to the developmental requirements of your soul.*

9. Life is Not Fair - *Each soul is challenged in ways unique to its own development. Some can handle tougher challenges than others.*

10. Law of Change – *If you want to get to a place or condition where you are not, you must be willing to change from where or what you are.*

Thus, concludes the first section of the manuscript. Carter enjoys discussing the ten translated laws of life at length with Professor Crozier.

After much thought, the professor says that he can now see how these principles have been at work in his life all along, and that knowing about them will allow him to make much better use of his remaining life.

The professor goes on to say, "According to this manuscript, life is a chance to improve our character by the way we interact with each other in everything we do."

"That seems to be what it says," agreed Carter. "We take from life no more than we bring into it except for the impact our actions have in shaping our eternal souls while we are here."

"These are some pretty profound statements. I can't wait to see what's in the rest of the document," says the professor. It is amazing how much better the wisdom in this ancient document can help us live as modern souls in our human bodies.

Carter says, "I will try to get back with you next weekend if you will be available."

"By all means," responds Professor Crozier, "this may be the most important document I ever translate!"

> "Hope arouses a passion for the possible."
> ...*Clergyman William S. Coffin, Jr.*

Out of suffering have emerged the most powerful souls.
...Philosopher Khalil Gibran

---

[1] W.B. Freeman Concepts, *God's Little Instruction Book on Character,* Honor Books, Tulsa, OK, 1996, p.32

[2] Caroline Myss, *Anatomy of the Spirit*, Crown Publishers, 1996, p.67

[3] Joyce Meyer, *Battlefield of the Mind,* Faith Words Hachette Book Group, 2011 p.66

[4] Charles Stanley broadcast 11/25/12

[5] Pastor Joel Osteen

Chapter 3

<u>Principles of Spiritual Being</u>

The **second section** of the manuscript from the Temple Mount in Jerusalem contains nine significant spiritual principles that can help us understand the process for the growth and transcendence of our human souls.

Carter and Professor Crozier discuss these laws and principles extensively while translating them and are surprised at their relevance and clarity.

"These laws and principles of the soul would seem to be of great benefit to mankind," says Dr. Crozier. "However," he adds, "the real challenge, as noted, is in living according to them more so than just understanding what they say."

Carter responds saying, "Nevertheless, the more we understand about the principles that govern our being the better our chances of properly aligning our conduct with the way we are designed."

Inquiringly, he adds, "I wonder how the ancient ones knew of these things; maybe they were given to Moses with the Ten Commandments and lost to history when Solomon's great temple in Jerusalem was twice destroyed leaving only the massive foundation known today as the Temple Mount."

> **"Let your soul stand cool and composed**
> **before a million universes."**
> *...Poet and Author Walt Whitman*

Human Spiritual Powers

The Babylonians destroyed the first temple in 586 B.C.E., said Carter. It was rebuilt on the same spot and destroyed again by the Romans in the year 70 in the first century of the Common Era.[1] It has never been rebuilt, but this original document was found in rubble from the temple itself.

The professor notes, "Throughout human history, our greatest thinkers have studied the work of those who lived before them. Many of them would then add an insight or so of their own to the growing body of human knowledge."

"Over the course of history," he says, "we have accumulated a great deal of knowledge about human beings and the physical world around us. However, one of the areas we know the least about is these matters of the soul.

Professor Crozier observes that what we do know comes from many sources including historical and religious documents like the Bible. Our knowledge also comes from many cultures such as the ancient Chinese philosopher and sage, Confucius, who taught many of the same things that ancient Greeks, Jews, Christians, Romans, Arabs and other civilizations have noted about human nature.

The professor adds that Confucius believed the evils confronting human beings were rooted in personal spiritual defilements such as selfishness, self-centeredness, greed, hatred and the love of power. He is reported to have said that we should develop a love of learning and that we must practice kindness, humility and sincerity while banishing rudeness, coarse expression and violence.

"I just wonder," says Dr. Crozier, "how much knowledge was lost through wars, natural disasters and accidents like the big library fire in Egypt. According to Roman stoic philosopher Seneca, up to 40,000 books (scrolls) were burned up when the great international library in Alexandria, Egypt caught fire."[2]

**Character cannot be developed in ease and quiet.
Only through experience of trial and suffering can the soul be strengthened, ambition inspired, and success achieved.**
...Deaf/Blind Author Helen Keller

Chapter 3 Principles of Spiritual Being

During a naval battle in 48 B.C.E. in the port of Alexandria, a large group of ships was set afire at the docks. The fire accidently spread to the greatest library of that era where priceless knowledge from antiquity was lost forever.

Carter says that it now seems like some scientists are groping in the dark and grasping at straws for any ungodly explanation for human life.

For example, he says, while at the airport waiting for a flight one day, I overheard a couple of aeronautical engineers talking about a big beautiful new supersonic airliner that was just then landing. One engineer related the following story to the other: "An intelligent looking woman tried to tell me airplanes were formed by accident without design.[3]

"She said that over millions of years, metallic ore gradually converted itself to steel and aluminum, then into sheets and slowly emerged from the ground and grew into the wings, body and tail of a great airplane."

"In another million years, she said the jet engines were formed and grew onto the wings. Over the next millennium the cockpit, interior seats, windows and aisles were formed by trial and error, she insisted."

"Finally, she claimed that the aviation electronics, control panels, landing gear and all the other millions of essential components of a modern airliner emerged exactly as needed through survival of the fittest until the mechanical marvel was fit to fly."

"Many people were realizing that no intelligent designer existed, she advised, and that everything began with a big explosion and evolved from there. When I told her, I designed aircraft for a living, she said I was deluded, ignorant and completely out of touch with reality!" Both aircraft designers got a good laugh over that, adds Carter.

As they begin to translate the next part of the ancient manuscript, Professor Crozier says, "people can be very smart and very ignorant at the same time."

"**Benefit yourself by benefiting others**."
...Oriental proverb

"Often," he adds, "it is because they have been culturally conditioned or brainwashed to believe only what fits with the current ideology."

The translated second section of the ancient manuscript is presented on the following pages:

Handbook of the Soul

Principles of Spiritual Being

I. Introduction

Spiritual growth and wisdom can be achieved by correcting character weaknesses that are most easily identified in the mysterious earthly laboratory of good, evil, temptation and uncertainty.

- *Character weaknesses are improved by learning to control your thoughts and by making better, less selfish, moral choices that replace vice with virtue.*

- *Both good and evil behaviors tend to further themselves, which is to say that virtue begets even more virtue and vice begets even more vice.*

We need more spiritual power.
...30th U.S. President Calvin Coolidge

- *We do not suffer punishment for breaking a vindictive God's laws. Instead, we are suffering from the growing pains of character development, inadequate self-control and an incomplete understanding of the spiritual laws, principles and powers a loving God built into our souls.*

- *Understanding the laws, principles and powers of human spirituality can help us make the very most of our earthly opportunities for spiritual growth and transformation.*

Preview: Nine operating Laws and principles of the human Soul

1. **The Principle of Moderation**
2. **The Law of Temper**
3. **The Principle of Seed, Time and Harvest**
4. **The Law of Sin and Death**
5. **The Law of External Influence**
6. **The Principle of Praise**
7. **The Law of Truth or Consequence**
8. **The Law of Reciprocity**
9. **The Principle of Gratitude**

II. The Important Laws and Principles of the Soul

1. **The Principle of Moderation** - *Moderation and balance are generally preferable to excess and extremes in most aspects of human behavior (except with regard to virtue where more is usually better).*

- *The application of restraint is a vital concept of the human will.*

- *Selfish, addictive, immoral, criminal or similarly unrestrained human behaviors result from inadequate self-control.*

A continuous pattern of these radical negative behaviors can degrade your character, reverse your spiritual development and affect your eternal destiny.

- *Practice everything in moderation (including moderation).*

- *Moderation has been called the "Golden Mean."*

2. **The Law of Temper** - *A failure to control your temper is a selfish, unrestrained behavior that if not corrected can lead to even more extreme violent, immoral or even criminal behavior.*

Temper is defined as a balance of qualities; quality of mind or spirit; the state of a substance or being; a characteristic cast of mind or state of feeling and disposition.

Your human disposition or temper is the temperature of your soul, a mental and emotional balance that must be maintained within acceptable limits.

- *When you lose your temper, you temporarily lose the balance and control of your soul.*

- *Uncontrolled anger can quickly lead to rage, which is a human soul in crisis that is completely out of control.*

- *Having a bad temper is something to be ashamed of, because it means you cannot control yourself in some situations.*

Even under stressful conditions, your temper is usually maintained with enough subconscious will power to confront automatically the emotional forces pushing you to a rise in anger.

At times, the forces leading to anger are stronger than your automatic control system. In such instances, your spirit, using courage, must immediately deploy enough will power to force your anger back under control.

- *Keep your mind serene and focused on the things that are most important in life.*

- *Losing your temper in anger and rage is a complete loss or breakdown of spiritual control.*

Keep your mind and body occupied with worthwhile activity, and do not allow laziness or boredom to take root in your soul.
...Evangelist Billy Graham

- *It is a very serious issue that must be controlled because, as with all situations involving a breakdown in spiritual control, **each episode eases the way for the next**.*

- *Uncontrolled anger ultimately leads to a cancer-like corruption of your soul.*

- *Weakened control of your soul can also result in serious addictions such as alcoholism, drug addiction and addiction to pornography, nicotine or gambling.*

The following steps are important ways to deal with the onset of anger and rage:

1. *Recognize the onset of anger as soon as possible.*

2. *Temporarily disengage from the activity causing the anger.*

3. *Take deep breaths, while actively working at calming yourself and re-asserting control.*

4. *Do ten quick repetitions of push-ups, sit-ups or jumping jacks.*

5. *Do something else to refocus the mind, like listen to your spouse or to catchy music.*

6. *Doing something for someone else or a pet is very effective.*

7. *After restoring calm and composure, return to the activity with determination not to lose control.*

8. *If the situation becomes so stressful that you start to lose control, walk away.*

9. *Ask yourself, if this activity really has to take place, and if so, can it be done another day?*

10. *Very often, the situation becomes less frustrating, and it can be handled better after a period of time.*

Taking off his glasses, Dr. Crozier says it's time for a break, "My eyes need a rest though I don't want to stop. Carter," he asks, "you are just a young man in your twenties. Why are you so interested in the human soul? "

"I don't know why," responds Carter, "but I am fascinated with all aspects of the human soul. My cousin, grandfather and I want to contribute to human knowledge of the soul, so we are compiling a book on everything we can find about it, including six specific questions about life for which we have been seeking answers.

I would be happy to show you the questions and our Handbook of the Soul if you like."

"I most certainly would like to see them. At this point in life, my soul is of utmost importance to me," replies the professor. "But first, let's finish translating the second section of this fascinating manuscript."

3. <u>The Principle of Seed, Time and Harvest</u> - *The human spiritual processes of change via thought, speech and action are gradual, have the most effect and produce the best results when applied with patience, persistence and consistency over time much like planting crops.*

The process follows the principle of seed, time and harvest, bearing fruit of the same variety when planted and nurtured consistently.

- *He, who would be blessed, let him scatter blessings. She, who would be happy let her consider the happiness of others. In life, we get by giving. We retain by sharing; we even invest our money (loan it out) to get it to grow.*

- *We cannot expect to sow the seeds of strife and discord in our thoughts and words without reaping the same in return.*

- *We can think and talk more of goodness and happiness and behave with generosity, and gratitude, and over time, it will come back to us.*

*Selfishness and judgementalism, on the other hand, beget self-centered unhappiness. Therefore, if that is your state in life, you might look **within** for the cause.*

**An angry person stirs up conflict,
and a hot-tempered person commits many sins.**
... Proverbs 29:22

If you are troubled, sorrowful, depressed and unhappy, ask yourself the following questions:

- *What mental seeds have you long been sowing?*

- *What have you done for others?*

- *What is your attitude toward gratitude? Are you thankful for what you have?*

- *What seeds of trouble, conflict and woe have you sown that you should reap these bitter weeds?*

You Harvest What You Plant *- If you find* **selfishness** *planted in your life, dig it up and plant* **selflessness** *instead. It will take a good deal of time to grow and time for the old weeds of selfishness to die out, but it will do so as surely as the years give way one to the next.*

- *It is this same spiritual principal that allows you to develop a favorable character trait or virtue over time by acting as you would act if you already owned that virtue.*

- *Sometimes, the only way to develop a quality is to begin to behave as if you already have it.*

For example, if you were feeling negative and depressed when you had to lead an important meeting, the best thing you could do would be to act in a positive enthusiastic manner that would help generate constructive, creative attitudes in others, and before you know it you will get caught up in the positive enthusiasm yourself.

4. **The Law of Sin and Death** *- Disordered desire or a failure of positive spiritual control resulting in negative, harmful or destructive behavior is often known as sin or vice. It is behavior most contrary to the wholesome virtue of God, and it turns our souls away from Him.*

We should be always in control of our thoughts and desires and masters of our wills while living with a quiet, unobtrusive dignity and consideration for others.

- *The nature of vice and sin slowly creates division and disintegration within our souls. It has the effect, by degree, of creating decay and weakness in your spiritual strength and character.*

- *Although not immediately perceptible to us, sin eventually results in internal chaos and it can be felt as unhappiness, or depression and a slide into more sin and possibly evil.*

- *Sins of commission are sinful actions taken such as lying, stealing, cheating and hurting or killing other people.*

- *Sins of omission are a result of not doing something that should be done, such as not helping another person in dire need of assistance, not paying taxes or not disciplining unruly children.*

- *Sin separates us from who we could be, from our families and friends; it can cause divorce, and it separates us from God.*

- *Significant unrepentant sin can ultimately lead to an earlier or more difficult death.*

5. The Law of External Influence - *Your thought patterns can be affected significantly by the type of input received via your eyes and ears.*

*Over time, the nature of the input from **friends** and **conversation**, can affect your unconscious perspective, attitude and outlook on life and the nature of your soul.*

- *Many people think about whatever comes into their minds based on what they hear, see and discuss.*

- *If you try hard enough, you can control the nature of your thinking especially if you avoid negative influences.*

Carter remarked about how much more **input** we have to contend with in modern music, television, books, news, movies, the internet and other digital electronic media.

"Some people are so fond of ill luck that they run halfway to meet it."
...Douglas Jerrold

- *Develop, therefore, the habit of carefully evaluating the friends and other people, experiences and information you allow into your life. Because, they affect your thinking and eventually, they affect the quality of your soul.*

- *More frequent exposure to positive or negative influence has a positive or negative effect respectively, on your consciousness and your spiritual character.*

- *Constant exposure to base, immoral, disrespectful or violent expression has a degenerative impact that should be avoided because it desensitizes your spirit to negative forces and behaviors that you should find revolting and unacceptable.*

*On the other hand, you can be a positive external influence on other people by being a voice of encouragement that builds them up whenever it is justified! It is unfortunate that we have become a nation of critics who are constantly putting others down, because **a critical spirit is a costly vice**.*

**The righteous should choose friends carefully, for
the way of the wicked leads them astray.**
...Proverbs 12:26

6. The Principle of Praise - *When we are in a struggle, and we think we can't go on, praising God can be a way to develop a breakthrough. One of the most effective ways to get our minds completely off ourselves is by giving our attention over to praising someone else. God is the most deserving of praise for the grace he has given us, so praising him makes the most sense. It also affirms your faith in him.*

- *The praise is not for God; because he is not so vain that he needs to hear it, however, it might be like the unusual experience of hearing our own children praise us.*

- *Instead, the praise benefits she who is praising, not he who is praised. It helps us rise above our circumstances when we can praise God in spite of our circumstances.*

- *The first and greatest commandment is to love thy God with all thy heart and all thy soul. Praise is a way of doing so.*

We should always have an attitude of love and respect for God, just as we would expect from our children who love us.

7. The Law of Truth or Consequence - *There are human consequences to poor choices.*

- *Although Divine forgiveness is available, we must live with the consequences of our choices in this lifetime.*

- *There are times in the life of every person who takes a stand on high moral principles when his or her faith in, and knowledge of, those principles will be tested to the utmost.*

- *The way in which we come out of the difficult trials affects whether we have sufficient spiritual strength to live as a being of truth, in the company of the liberated, or remain a slave to the cruel taskmaster of our own fear and selfish desires.*

- *Such trials generally assume the form of temptation to do a wrong thing and gain comfort and prosperity, or stand by what is right and accept possible poverty and failure. Spiritually strong and virtuous must they be who can come triumphant out of such a trial.*

- *They who come triumphant out of such a trial enter into a higher realm of life where their spiritual eyes are opened wider because with some selfishness overcome, human insight into truth is clearer, and the poverty and ruin that seemed inevitable does not come.*

- *Likewise, ultimate prosperity comes not for those who consistently yield to temptation and make the wrong choices.*

- *Unbroken calm in the face of all outward antagonism is the dependable indication of a self-conquered soul in possession of wisdom and truth.*

8. The Law of Reciprocity - *Sometimes known as "what goes around comes around"- If you are feeling depressed and discouraged, one of the best ways to bring yourself out of it is to encourage someone else.*

- *Doing something for someone else is a sure cure for what ails us.*

- *Cheering an unhappy friend usually results in two cheerful souls.*

- *Volunteering to help others will defeat loneliness and a host of other personal problems. Make it a regular priority to help others in some way each day.*

9. <u>The Principle of Gratitude</u> – *Living with an **attitude of gratitude** can make a tremendous difference in the whole tone of your life. All of us have much to be thankful for, even though we do have the challenges and problems that partly define us. Most important is the divine grace that lets us keep trying to reform our souls despite repeated shortcomings.*

The interesting thing about this principle is that a soul's attitude of gratitude tends to open it up to more blessing and opportunities. It is as if true gratitude triggers an expansion of the soul's capacity to receive properly.

- *No one has even close to all the possible human problems, sicknesses and difficulties at once. No matter what your circumstances, they could be worse.*

- *An attitude of gratitude is a mindset of appreciation for what you have and for the things people do for you, especially your loved ones. It's easy to take so very much for granted including people who care about us.*

We could be enjoying and delighting in all that we have, instead of focusing on what we want but don't have.

- *All these riches are so much more valuable and enjoyable for those who continue to appreciate them deeply and daily.*

- *A soul that wakes up each day truly thankful to God for its many blessings gets to enjoy life so much more than one who focuses on the getting but not the having.*

> **"No matter how dark things seem to be, raise your sights and see possibilities, always see them, for they are always there."**
> *...Motivational Speaker Norman Vincent Peale*

- *Obviously, the hut, cattle and clothes care not that you appreciate them, so what matters is the impact of an appreciative attitude on your own soul.*

- *Being intentionally and continuously thankful for the people, conditions and things in your life reflects back on you. And, it shapes your soul a little closer to a right relationship with the Divine, while easing the path of your journey on Earth.*

III. Summary

Spiritual growth and wisdom can be achieved by correcting character weaknesses that are most easily identified in the mysterious earthly laboratory of good, evil, temptation and uncertainty.

- *Character weaknesses are improved by learning to control your thoughts and by making better, less selfish, moral choices that replace vice with virtue.*

- *Both good and evil behaviors tend to further themselves, which is to say that virtue begets even more virtue and vice begets even more vice.*

Understanding laws and principles of the human soul and putting them to work in your life can help you make the very most of your earthly opportunities for character development and spiritual transformation.

Humanity does not suffer punishment for breaking a vindictive God's laws; humanity instead is suffering from character flaws, lack of self-control and ignorance of the spiritual laws of a loving God.

IV. Review

This chapter covered the following laws and principles of Spiritual Being:

1. **The Principle of Moderation** - *Practice everything in moderation (including moderation)*

> "We are not simply bystanders on a cosmic stage,
> but shapers and creators living in a participatory universe."
> *...Theoretical Physicist John Wheeler*

2. The Law of Temper – *Control anger in the soul, for each episode eases the way for the next.*

3. The Principle of Seed, Time and Harvest – *A gradual processes of spiritual change reaping what we sow.*

4. The Law of Sin and Death – *Sin or vice leads to destructive behavior and self-inflicted wounds of the soul.*

5. The Law of External Influence - *Human thought patterns are affected by external input.*

6. The Principle of Praise - *Praising God is a way to affirm faith in him.*

7. The Law of Truth or Consequence – *To poor choices there are human consequences.*

8. The Law of Reciprocity - *What goes around comes around in the way we treat others.*

9. The Principle of Gratitude - *An attitude of gratitude erodes selfishness and improves spiritual progress.*

Carter said a modern version of the passage on gratitude might be to develop an attitude of gratitude, by stopping and thinking often about how neat it is to have a car when you start yours, the TV when you turn it on and your spouse when you turn him or her on.

Sometimes when you use them, think how really cool it is to have hot and cold running water, a refrigerator, microwave, dishwasher, washing machine and dryer.

Professor Crozier agreed and was thinking about how much harder life would be without the modern conveniences. He replied that we appreciate electricity most right after the power goes out.

With each storm of cold wind and rain, we ought to glance at the ceiling and walls of our houses and thank God, we live in a prosperous time and place where we can earn enough for a good house in which to live.

And now I exhort you to be of good cheer.
...Acts 27:22

Human Spiritual Powers

The professor added that we live in one of the richest countries in history and live better, by far, than most of the seven billion people on earth. Kings and Queens of old didn't live as well as we do today.

Carter suggested they consider for a moment some things that are usually taken for granted:

- abundant food and water
- adequate housing
- more than one set of clothes and shoes
- good hospitals, doctors and medicine
- free public education, freedom and democracy
- fantastic music and endless entertainment
- good working conditions and cool transportation
- money to spend, places to shop
- peace and personal security in most places

The professor, thinking about some of the places he had seen in his travels, remarked that you could be homeless, and strung out on drugs.

Alternatively, you could be living with constant pain from an incurable disease that is slowly killing you and your loved ones.

Worse yet, you could be an addict or a jobless invalid suffering from serious depression and all manner of diseases in a country with only witchdoctors.

Carter learned a great deal from the ancient manuscript and his discussions with Professor Crozier about the evident wisdom it contained.

They were both amazed at how the principles and powers were as relevant today and perhaps more important than they were when they were written so many centuries ago.

The thing Carter liked most was that each item was clearly and concisely written and easy to understand. It helped him clarify his own thinking about the whole concept of the principles of spiritual power.

They even thought that perhaps the ancient manuscript was part of the legendary "Wisdom of Solomon."

Professor Crozier noted that some ancient Greek influence including some of Aristotle and perhaps Plato's rational thinking seemed to be involved in the document's wisdom.

In business with his partners, Carter was soon making plenty of money for all of them. However, his real interest and curiosity were concerned with the average people, their activities, petty worries, pleasures and acts of foolishness.

However easily he succeeded in talking to them, in living with them, in learning from them, he was still aware that there was something, which separated him from them, and this separating factor was Carter still being at heart an Ascetic and a spiritual pilgrim.

He saw mankind going through life in a childlike or animal like manner. He saw them toiling, saw them suffering, and becoming weak for the sake of things which seemed to him to be entirely unworthy of this price: for money, for status symbols and for security that does not exist.

He saw them scolding and insulting each other and gossiping and putting one another down, griping, moaning and groaning about their circumstances and feeding on bad news like vampires on blood.

He saw them overeating, then heard them complaining about joint pains at which an Ascetic would only smile. He saw them suffering from deprivations which an Ascetic would not even notice.

At times Carter felt, deep in his chest, a dying voice, which admonished him and lamented so quietly that he hardly perceived it. Occasionally he became aware of the strange life he was leading, of doing lots of things that were only a game to him while real life was still passing him by and not really touching him.

**Where there is no divine revelation,
people cast off restraint, but blessed is the one who heeds wisdom.**
...Proverbs 29:18

He wished that he would be able to participate in all of these naive-childlike human activities with passion and drama, really to live, to cut loose, to enjoy life's many pleasures and to be happy and sad like others instead of just moving through life as a professional observer.

But again, and again, he came back to his conversations with Brenda and Carolyn who, like Warden, were interested in the same things he was: The great themes of life and duty, and the eternal questions of humanity."

This is what is most important to Carter because men and women have been confused forever about the meaning of life, the existence and role of the soul and even about the existence of God.

> **"Everyone thinks of changing the world, but**
> **no one thinks of changing himself"**
> *...Russian author Leo Tolstoy*

Brenda once said, "Many people are like a falling leaf, which is blown and is turning around through the air, and wavers, and eventually tumbles to the ground because people are anxious, and lack faith in God." "Mankind," she said, "truly perishes from a lack of faith."

Carter recalls hearing that the three most important spiritual decisions humans must make are the:

1. Decision to have faith in Divinity

2. Decision to change from vice and sin

3. Decision to forgive others

> **"Never undertake anything for which you wouldn't have**
> **the courage to ask the blessings of heaven."**
> *...Georg Christoph Lichtenberg*

---

[1] Gafni, Isaiah M.; The Teaching Company 2003; Course "Great World Religions: Judaism"

[2] Seneca, *De Tranquillitate Animi (On Tranquility of Mind)*

[3] R.A. Laidlaw, *The Reason Why, Executive* Books, Mechanicsburg, PA, 2002, p.9

Chapter 4

<u>Spiritual Powers</u>

Meeting weekends, Carter and Professor Crozier continue to bring back to life the long dead words of the manuscript from the Temple Mount in Jerusalem. Carter is surprised at how much he enjoys helping translate the document.

APOLLYON continues to harass the more outspoken leaders of organized religion and anyone who supports them. Therefore, Carter asks Professor Crozier if he knows why APOLLYON is so against religion.

The professor replies that many of the leaders of APOLLYON are atheists who hate the concept of a God or religions that might preach against their lifestyles.

Furthermore, he says Socialists and Communists hate religions because they teach that God instead of the government is the highest power on which people should depend. Religion also affirms that there are certain God given human rights that should protect citizens from torture or other acts of extreme government control.

Your immortal soul is made in the likeness of God. It is more valuable than all the stars and planets in the universe put together.
...Author Anthony De Stefano

The Socialists want to be able to force people to do what the government wants them to do, whether the people like it or not. Threatening, jailing and killing people gives governments absolute power to do whatever they want.

That kind of absolute power, he says, has led to the combined, documented deaths of over 100 million people, in Socialist Nazi Germany, Communist China and the Communist Soviet Union including my own parents. People try to flee from these kinds of countries, and every year many are killed trying to escape to freedom. APOLLYON wants absolute power in this country, so they are trying to discredit religion as one obstacle to it.

The **third section** of the manuscript explains that in the realm of the soul, we are invested with great and awesome **spiritual powers** to help us combat the challenges of life that we face on Earth. Sometimes we take them for granted or do not even recognize them for the powerful weapons they are. However, like most weapons we must understand how they work and practice with them to become truly proficient in their application.

<u>Handbook of the Soul</u>

Spiritual Powers

Spiritual evolution is part of every soul's destiny on earth, and each soul grows and evolves at a different rate. Are you where you need to be?

I. Preview

*The following dozen spiritual powers, **when properly understood**, can help fulfill our spiritual destiny by giving us tremendous authority over the challenges of human life. These powers may seem simple in comparison to powers of great physical force; however, these spiritual powers are, in the grand scheme of things, more powerful than erupting volcanoes.*

Physical force is limited to the physical dimensions of existence, while the much more important force of spiritual power holds far greater meaning across all times and dimensions. This chapter covers the following commanding spiritual powers available to all Human beings:

1. *The Power of Faith*
2. *The Power of Imagination and Positive Imaging*
3. *The Power of Prayer*
4. *The Power to Choose*
5. *The Power of Self-discipline*
6. *The Power of Thought*
7. *The Power of Confession and Repentance*
8. *Power Projection and Confirming Action*
9. *The Power of Intention and Commitment*
10. *The Power of Forgiveness*
11. *The power of Patience*
12. *The Power of Courage*

II. Powers of the Spirit

1. <u>The Power of Faith</u>: *Faith is the belief and trust in God; based on spiritual conviction rather than proof. Faith, the opposite of fear, is an extremely powerful spiritual force capable of freeing you from negative forces of fear, worry, doubt and sickness.*

- *Faith is said to be the substance of things hoped for; the evidence of things not yet seen.*

- *Faith is a bridge between the objective, and scientifically observable facts of physical life and the subjective, invisible and equally true facts of spiritual life.*

A faith that has been tested can be trusted.
...Writer and Pastor Adrian Rogers

Human Spiritual Powers

*It is only through eyes of faith that spiritual truths can be truly understood. Therefore, we must have the **faith to believe**, so that we may come **to understand** that which is invisible to our physical senses. This has come to be known as the "leap of faith" that is necessary to bridge the gap between two kinds of truth: physical and spiritual.*

- *Faith can be considered a leap from spiritual darkness into spiritual light.*

- *Faith is a potent spiritual discipline of the soul, and it must be trained and practiced to be effective.*

- *Faith should eventually cause you to act differently than before you found faith.*

Faith in God *- does not necessarily come with a sudden intuitive leap of understanding, or a striking occurrence; it can occur slowly and gradually deepen, as you **will your soul** to accept Divine reality and your spiritual existence as a spark thereof.*

Divine Faith is composed of the following three elements:

1. **Trust** – the trust that God is an all-powerful, loving God of grace and forgiveness who is pulling for you to transform your soul successfully through the process of this life.

2. **Loyalty** – the loyalty to put your **ultimate, sacred, cosmic** trust in God and not in physical things such as money, government, other people or false gods.

3. **Compliance** – the willingness to help God help you, by living in right, prayerful and spiritual relationship with Him, while trying to live a just, honorable, respectful and unselfish physical life with other people.

Negate Your Soul - *Living in wrong relationship with God weakens your soul. However, living a life of faith (trust, loyalty and compliance) will put you in right relationship with God greatly assisting you in life's central purpose, which is the challenging spiritual process of transforming your soul.*

The act of faith is a decision, not a feeling.

Chapter 4 Spiritual Powers

*God relates to Human Beings through His **grace**. Human beings relate to God via **faith**. God's grace is free, but it will not help you very much if you do not have enough faith to believe God exists in the first place. In addition, you must believe that you are deserving of and are covered by God's grace.*

*__Faith Is Like Oxygen and Food__ - Oxygen and food are all around us, and we must have plenty of them to live our best lives. However, we must **breathe in the air** and **eat the food** for them to be of any help! Likewise, we must internalize faith into our souls to become the best we can be.*

You can develop faith by prayer, reading and thinking about spiritual things, speaking and behaving like you have faith and you love God and are trying to follow his directions.

__Give Faith Time__ - It may take some time, so you must be patient and give faith time to take root and grow. This could be a matter of months or years depending on your personal level of commitment. You could soon come to a place where peace gradually replaces anxiety, as prayer becomes a regular part of your life.

As far as a belief that you may not deserve God's grace, it may help you to remember the following:

1. *Justice is **getting** what we **deserve**; (the painful consequences of selfish, fearful ways)*

2. *Mercy is **not getting** what we deserve. (which is a very negative spiritual transformation)*

3. *Grace is getting what we **don't** deserve. (God's love, forgiveness and encouragement)*

*__From Within__ - However, as much as God may love, forgive and encourage us and offer his grace; it is only we who can accept it and can reform and transform our own souls; for the spiritual transformation must come from **within** each of us as part of an inner shift in character for it to be effective.*

"Our faith is God's conduit to us for forgiveness and goodness."
...Pastor Robert Jeffress

Human Spiritual Powers

<u>People of Faith</u> - *Associate with people of faith, listen to and tell decent, uplifting stories and sing uplifting songs (modern translation watch and listen to decent, positive material instead of music and movies filled with strife, sex and violence).*

- *You can be successful if you do these things and avoid the negative behaviors that bring ill to yourself and others.*

- *Treat other people, as you would like to be treated. Lift people up, in every way, every day.*

<u>God Between</u> - *Some people feel that they don't deserve God's grace, but they would be well advised to let Him be the judge of that and accept His grace with the honor and dignity it deserves.*

- *God expects to be first in your life, to be whom you depend on most for life and security.*

- *A milestone of spiritual understanding is the realization that **faith puts God between you and your problems.***

<u>Shallow Faith</u> – *True faith in a powerful, gracious God would not result in the kind of behavior often exhibited by those of shallow faith and mere religious opinion.*

- *They quickly give way to complaint, despondency and grief as soon as some petty trouble overtakes them.*

- *Those given to irritability, anxiety, lamentation and hopelessness over the problems of life should know that real, deep faith produces courage, fortitude steadfastness and the strength to better face life's problems, many of which will still challenge us.*

<u>Live Honorably</u> - *If we develop the faith to receive God's grace, that same faith condition will also cause us to want to live honorably. We do not do good things and live right to earn God's grace for the simple reason that you cannot earn what is freely given, but you do live right to be worthy of that grace.*

"Faith is knowledge within the soul, beyond the reach of proof."
...Philosopher Khalil Gibran

Chapter 4 Spiritual Powers

<u>Worthy</u> - *when you have taken the step of faith it takes to believe God exists and that you are covered by his grace, then as you grow in prayer and faith you will want to become worthy of the grace, faith and confidence God has in you by living a decent, unselfish and honorable life. You will also come to realize that doing so, really doing so, will greatly improve your life and set you on the mystical path to a complete spiritual transformation. You should, therefore, feed your faith and starve your fears.*

For Five Steps to Faith and Dealing with Doubt see the appendix following this chapter on page 93.

2. <u>The Power of Imagination and Positive Imaging</u> - *Your imagination is the creative engine of your being that can affect your attitude positively or negatively.*

Thinking, speaking, imagining and envisioning things as they could be, with unrelenting faith that they will be, can generate spiritual power, which coupled with physical action, greatly enhances the chance of success in any human endeavor.

- *It has been said that imagi**nation** is the most powerful nation on earth. Therefore, we must make it our ally not our enemy.*

- *As our ally, our imagination creates opportunity, but as our enemy, it creates worry, stress, fear and self-defeat.*

Although you cannot directly determine your circumstances, you can indirectly, but surely, influence your circumstances by carefully choosing your thoughts.

- *All that you accomplish and all that you fail to accomplish will depend first and foremost on your thoughts.*

- *Aspects of what you most believe can eventually come to pass in your life. Therefore, we must be careful to believe in positive, goodness, mercy, love and the grace of God.*

Life makes you or breaks you, as you choose.
...Unknown

Positive Affirmation - *Stating your goals as if they have been met already and reaffirming them often sets loose the power of positive affirmation.*

- *It has been said that if we could fill our minds with only good and expect only good, then good would more likely come to us.*

- *In the proportion that sin, fear and evil are in our thoughts, so will more trouble inevitably be in our lives.*

Inner Posture - *The outward circumstances of your life depend on the inner posture, condition and reality of your consciousness.*

- *That which you desire in life, you must first build into your consciousness.*

- *If you can conceive it and believe it, you can often achieve it, if you work hard enough at it (unless you are trying to contradict the laws of nature).*

Controlling Consciousness and its Thought - *is said to be the secret of life! As your consciousness changes, so may the outer conditions of your life.*

The way to success, peace, harmony, abundance, love and health is first to establish these things in your consciousness by thinking positively, studying scripture and other positive material.

- *__Thinking__ continuously about the good you desire and the good you can do and affirming it in prayer.*

- *Truly __believing__ that God is working with you, guiding you, strengthening you and facilitating your way forward toward improved character and the good you seek in life.*

- *Even in a busy neighborhood, you are more likely to find a parking space for your chariot if you're looking for one.*

- *Having deep and optimistic hope keeps possibilities alive in our minds, so if even obscure opportunities arise, having them in mind helps us more readily recognize and act on them.*

Think not on failure and negativity, but decide how blessed you are and be __thankful__ for it.

Chapter 4 Spiritual Powers

"Let's take a break," says the Professor, "translating this is very hard work. No, never mind, I just can't wait to see what else is in this amazing document."

3. The Power of Prayer - *Prayer can greatly strengthen and energize your spirit, and it can bring peace to your soul.*

- *Prayer is one of the most effective ways to deal with the challenges and opportunities of human life.*
- *Prayer is the way to keep your soul connected with God.*
- *Prayer and meditation are the best ways to improve your spiritual consciousness.* (Book 4 covers prayer.)

4. The Power to Choose - *As a human being, through the exercise of your **free will**, you have the power to choose and control the nature of your own thought, speech and activities.*

- ***Choose Input*** - *You also have extensive freedom to choose the positive or negative nature of the external input you receive through your eyes and ears and the kind of people with whom you hang out.*

- ***Choices Impact*** - *These choices can greatly impact your character development and, therefore, the course of your human and subsequent existence.*

- ***Genetic Independence*** - *The awesome power of your free will or freedom to choose must be nurtured and taught to assert itself by seeking truth and becoming more independent of your genetic tendencies and predispositions.*

- ***Will's Freedom*** - *Developing your **will's** freedom is an accomplishment that increases your capacity for choosing how you want to spend your time and other resources.*

Will to Choose Wisely - *Developing your **will** can allow you to rise above the animal instincts of your being to assert well-reasoned preferences, which become an indication of what you love.*

Willpower is one of the greatest possessions we have, the challenge is to maintain a strong will and yet be humble and teachable.
...Author Gene A. Getz

Human Spiritual Powers

- ***Gift and Curse*** - *Elisabeth Kubler-Ross has said that mankind's greatest gift, and also our greatest curse, is that we have free choice. We can make our choices based on love or on fear.*

- ***Choose Wisely*** - *Although human beings can benefit from a social structure that helps us learn to restrain our base desires, it remains each individual's responsibility to attain wisdom by training his or her own **will** to choose wisely.*

- ***Good or Bad*** - *One of humanity's strongest powers is our willpower, however, if misused, it can be powerfully bad instead of powerfully good.*

Bad Things to Good People - *Why does God allow so many bad, negative and unfair things to happen, and why doesn't he just blast all evil away? (Or at least tell all mankind, in a completely clear and unmistakable way, the truth about life after death and what he wants us to do here on earth.)*

The answer is that God could physically appear to all humanity in such a way that his very presence would scare, intimidate or coerce humans into doing the right things whether they want to or not.

*In that way, everyone would do the right things only because they would be **afraid** to do anything wrong.*

Unfortunately, the result would eliminate free human will and with it the opportunity for true spiritual growth that comes with learning to change our desires.

*The positive development of the human soul requires **desiring** to act righteously as a result of the development of our own **spiritual convictions**, as opposed to just being afraid to misbehave or do whatever we might really desire to do.*

Limited Physical Presence - *God has mostly chosen to stay in the background and limit his physical presence in such a way that he can sometimes respond to sincere prayer, but without controlling or coercing human spiritual development in the process.*

"The living soul of man, once conscious of its power, cannot be quelled."
... Educator Horace Mann

Chapter 4 Spiritual Powers

Difficult to prove- *Perhaps that is why it is so difficult to prove scientifically the existence of God.*

- **_Absence of Certainty_** - *The earthly experience provides temptation, doubt and the absence of eternal certainty that requires you to exercise the freedom of choice necessary for your spiritual development.*

- **_No Compulsion_** - *Without the physical certainty of God, or eternal truth and knowledge, there is no intimidation, pressure or compulsion to righteous behavior that could preclude true human choice.*

  - **_True Nature_** - *So, in the earthly fog of eternal uncertainty, each human soul chooses its thoughts and actions more in accord with the true nature of its own developing spiritual character.*

  - **_Your Choice_** - *At the same time, thanks to God's grace, you have the opportunity to improve your spiritual character through your choices, without being compelled to do so.*

  - **_Internal Conviction_** - *Real, genuine human righteousness, goodness and spiritual development cannot be coerced or forced; it must come about through the free choice, internal conviction and personal desire of each individual.*

Unfettered choice allows for the very important distinction between becoming truly good of your own accord, as opposed to behaving in good ways for other reasons.

No One Looking - *In other words, you must develop the spiritual character to do what is right, because it is right, even if no one else is looking and even if there were no other positive or negative consequences involved.*

Being forced or coerced into goodness prevents you from ever truly learning to choose good verses bad, or right instead of wrong.

**God gives us enough evidence
to convince, but not enough to coerce.**
...Philosopher & Theologian Peter Kreeft

Human Spiritual Powers

- ***Un-coerced*** - *Ultimately, it is the completely voluntary improvement of internal spiritual character born of a free will and the un-coerced desire to act with discipline, love and acceptance that is most important for the spiritual development that will allow us to move forward after life in this dimension.*

- ***Uncontrolled Environment*** - *The development of your soul might not be possible except in an uncontrolled environment of temptation and opportunity that allows you to make good or bad choices for yourself (conditions of life on earth).*

- ***Absence*** - *The development of faith in God can occur only in the absence of God's visible presence.*

With free will, the decision to pursue truth and the choice to adopt, practice and master good and righteous behavior is, each and every minute of each and every day, the individual choice of each and every human soul.

"Wow, that sure tells it like it is," said Carter. "It's kind of amazing that we really are "spiritual free agents" in every sense of the word!"

5. The Power of Self-discipline – *Self-discipline is the means by which human beings can move themselves from the animal phase of subsistence through dualism to the ultimate and divine phase of existence.* [1]

Discipline must begin in the soul, for an ordered mind is necessary to an ordered life. Therefore, use your will to bring your passions and emotions under the control of your mind and spirit.

- ***Noble Qualities*** - *If you reach the stage of dualism and its awareness of the divine, you can first begin to aspire to the nobler qualities of life instead of simply living a cycle of sensual gratification and suffering.*

- ***Rein in Desires*** - *Using self-discipline, you can rein in the steed of your desires and begin to adjust your conduct to the dictates of reason and wisdom.*

Great are those who see that the spiritual is stronger than any material force, and that thoughts rule the world.
...Writer Ralph Waldo Emerson

Chapter 4 Spiritual Powers

- **Shape Destiny** - *Your progress will begin to take you from a life without meaning and purpose to one of consciously influencing your own destiny.*

You begin to discipline yourself by asserting control over feelings that have hitherto controlled you. Like athletes lifting weights to build muscles, we need challenges and problems in life to push back against in order to develop the virtuous muscles of self-control that are necessary to discipline our souls.

<u>Check Tongue</u> - *You put a check on your tongue, your temper and your appetite; and you begin to moderate all the lusts and desires that may have formerly dominated you.*

<u>Re-route</u> - *You do so by re-routing them from mindless, instinctive behavior to mindful actions that must gain permission from your mind to go forward.*

<u>*Two-step Improvement Process*</u>

*First, you must **think often** enough about the character trait or vice you wish to improve to cause a twinge of your conscience or a mental alert to occur whenever a relevant decision or choice arises involving the vice you are trying to eliminate.*

- *This first step may take a period of several weeks depending on how often each day you think about your goal.*

- *The second step is to **change behavior** as a result of the mental alerts or twinges of conscience.*

- *For example, if selfishness and pride were the vices you wanted to change, you should start thinking, off and on for weeks, about the need to be less self-centered and prideful.*

- *After thinking about your goal for a while, you should start getting vague mental suggestions from your conscience, perhaps while talking with friends, that you should consider saying something complimentary to lift up someone else for a change.*

"My father always said that what we think is what we become."
…*British Prime Minister Margaret Thatcher*

Human Spiritual Powers

As you **practice self-control**, you are less and less driven by selfish motives and fear, pleasure and pain.

- True strength and spiritual power are born of self–purification as you transmute the lower animal forces of your nature into intellectual and spiritual energy.

- The final stage of self–discipline is a process of pushing the inferior desires and all selfish appetites completely out of your mind.

Sacred Aspiration - Eventually, through thoughtful conduct, earnest meditation and sacred aspiration you will be able to prevent the selfish passions and desires from arising altogether.

Less Contaminated - As you grow less contaminated, you realize that wickedness is powerless against you unless it receives your encouragement, so disregard it and let it pass out of your life.

To the extent you desire, you can live a steadfast and virtuous life of strength, peace and fortitude. Thus purified, you can begin to enjoy a more peaceful soul and spiritually driven conduct.

- With self-discipline and hard work, you can attain every degree of education and prosperity, virtue and holiness and finally become a soul of more divine character.

- Without self-discipline, you drift lower and lower becoming more and more like a beast until at last you grovel as a lost creature living in the spiritual filth of your own sin and vice.[2]

6. The Power of Thought

- As a being of thought, your dominant mental attitude will determine your condition in life, and it will be the measure of your attainment. You are the thinker of your thoughts and as such you are the maker of yourself, your condition and to some extent your circumstances.

- Your attitude will color any situation or circumstance as dark and foreboding or bright and enlightening; and the great thing about it is that you have the choice of which it shall be.

Whatever people do, they must do first in their minds.
...Albert Szent -GyŐrgyi

- *Do you see difficulty in every opportunity or opportunity in every difficulty?*

- *You have the power to respond favorably or react negatively to any situation; however, reacting negatively clouds thinking, while responding positively creates opportunity.*

- *Thought is causal and creative; the harmonies and the antagonisms in your life are often the responsive echoes of your predominant thoughts.*

- *Anger, bitterness and resentment interfere with the body's healing process. (Modern translation: I don't eat junk food, and I don't think junk thoughts!)*

- *If your dominant mental attitude is gracious, unselfish and loving, more serenity and joy will follow you; if it be negative, selfish, contentious and resentful, more trouble and strife will cloud your path.*

- *Out of ill will, comes conflict and adversity; out of good will, peace, fellowship and harmony. Adopt a true attitude of gratitude and more abundance will come your way.*

*This day we are where our thoughts have **brought us**; we will be in the future where our thoughts **take us**. By altering our thoughts, we can, in time, alter our condition.[3]*

*When you can control your thoughts, you are a very **powerful being**; one of a tiny few that, over time, can determine its own state and much of its circumstance. Consider always into whose hands your thoughts are commending your soul.*

7. <u>The Power of Confession and Repentance</u> - *We are all guilty of transgressions, but we have been given the power to repair and reverse much of the internal damage our destructive behavior has on our souls with the powers of confession and repentance.*

Corrupt Activity - *If you are responsible for negative, corrupt activity, you must seek the forgiveness of God, and anyone harmed by your negative behavior.*

Repentance is a change of mind that leads to a change in conduct.

- *In prayer, you must sincerely acknowledge your failure.*

- *You must be genuinely sorry for the mistake with no intention of repeating it.*

Desire to Change - **Repentance** *is simply recognition of error and desire for change and improvement. God is aware of our errors, but are we willing to own up to them and improve?*

- *Recognition of error and desire to change are very important steps in the process of character development and spiritual transformation.*

- *If you fool yourself into believing your own failures are the fault of others, and you will not accept the truth, then you are one who is unrepentant or unwilling to change.*

- *Don't expect God to cover what you won't uncover by simply confessing to God your transgressions with sincere desire to change.[4] God already knows of our transgressions so it is only our willingness to confess and change that matters.*

Confession Reclaims - *The act of confession reclaims our spirits from negative thoughts and events past and present.*

- *Repentance reclaims that part of our spiritual energy that was invested in past fear and negativity.*

- *Remaining attached to negative events, beliefs and a negative attitude is toxic to our minds, spirits, cellular tissue and toxic to our lives in general.*

Willingness to Change - *Your own process of spiritual transformation will be restricted by the extent to which you remain unwilling to change.*

- *You must recognize your faults as the first step in purging them from your soul, and you must accept that you have these shortcomings before you can possibly begin to correct them.*

**"The moment one definitely commits oneself,
providence moves too, resulting in all manner of unforeseen assistance,
which no one could have dreamed would come his or her way."**
...W.H. Murray

- *Excessive pride and massive self-centeredness are often at the core of an unrepentant soul.*

- *Sadly, many arrogant people think they are much too sophisticated to believe in God, virtue or repentance.*

8. Power Projection and Confirming Action - *The power projection modes of your human consciousness are **thought**, **speech** and **physical action**.*

*__Affect Reality__- As previously noted, the nature of the **thought** that you **dwell upon** within your mind over time will affect your attitude, your speech, your choices, and your actions. It will eventually affect the reality of your circumstances and your habits and ultimately the spiritual character of your being.*

__Affirm Positive__ - If you think, speak and respond most often in a positive way, employing in your behaviors the positive modes of life (such as joy, harmony, faith, compassion etc.) these positive forces increasingly will come to predominate, affirming a positive spiritual character and improving your life.

__Reinforce Spirit__ - The positive thought and activity will, over time, strengthen and reinforce the positive nature of your spirit reflecting favorably, as well, upon your soul and the health of your physical body. Speaking with a positive attitude also has a favorable impact on family, friends and associates.

__Negative Afflicts__ - Likewise frequent negative thought, speech and action relating, for instance, to resentment, sorrow, anxiety, fear and strife will eventually afflict the body, soul and spirit that dwells upon it, just as the wheels of a cart must follow the feet of the ox that pulls it.

- *Constant exposure to negativity erodes your spiritual strength and debilitates your being.*

- *Frequently speaking and behaving in a negative manner reveals the ugly underbelly of your character and has a negative influence on those with whom you associate.*

Human Spiritual Powers

Quality of Your Soul - *You must come to understand the creative power of your thoughts and the impact of your spoken words and make every effort to discipline your mind and tongue. You should operate with the positive forces of life, and avoid the ever-present temptations of fear, selfishness, criticism and negativity because your thoughts, words and actions are determining the quality of your soul.*

Power of Confirming Action - *The human creative powers in faith, thought, speech and prayer are confirmed and reinforced in the strongest sense when you take **physical action** to affirm or bring about the **desired result**. Good **thoughts still take positive action** to bring them to **reality**.*

*To make the most progress in this life, you must make the **physical effort** necessary to produce the good things about which you believe, think, speak and pray.*

Many people move along the path of life motivated by the blind impulse of their untrained thinking as it is stimulated by desire, people and circumstances. Being ignorant of their spiritual nature, they become slaves of their undisciplined thinking habits and their resulting activities.

According to philosopher James Allen:

- *"The **spiritually wise** and disciplined thinker proceeds intelligently along the virtuous path of his own choosing in control of noble thoughts and compassionate actions."*

- *The **foolish**, thinking most often of their immediate pleasures, become victims of their own foolish thoughts and actions.*

- *"The foolish pursue an immoral, unrighteous, ultimately sorrowful and disturbed lifestyle because that is what they think about and act out."*

*Allen further observed that the **wise** and the **foolish** are **separated only** by their **differing thoughts**. Fortunately, the foolish can become wise by changing their thinking, but it becomes more difficult with age as old habits die hard. Every decision starts you down one pathway and away from others.*

**"Whether you think you can, or think you can't,
you're probably right!"**
...Automotive Pioneer Henry Ford

9. <u>The Power of Intention and Commitment</u> - *One of the best ways to influence the way your life unfolds is with the powers of intention and commitment.*

- *You can significantly improve your chances of success in whatever you choose to do by first being very clear in your mind and persistent about the outcomes you visualize.*

- *The very best way to **clarify your intentions** is to write down a short list of your most important goals.*

Simply list the top three or more short term goals that might take up to 3 years to achieve; the top three or more medium term goals 3 to 10 years to attain; and the top three long term goals that might take from 10 years to a lifetime to achieve.

- *The very **act of writing goals** down on paper is a powerful, committing force.*

- *Don't be afraid to start or get hung up on details.*

- *It doesn't need to be perfect; some people start on the back of a napkin, just writing things they want to do in their lives.*

*Think about it from time to time and get it roughed out and written up and use it as a map to guide some of your activity. It can be enjoyable, and it helps provide something of a **personal anchor** to add some stability to your life in our society of rapidly accelerating change.*

- *Some conditions will change, causing you to reevaluate your priorities.*

- *In many ways, you can affect conditions through your level of focus and commitment.*

- *You do not want to go through life adrift and blowing in the wind without developed character, values or goals.*

Your goals, objectives and some idea of how to attain them can be like a blueprint for your life. The following are examples of short, medium and long-term goals that you should change to fit your own preferences.

**"Stand up to your obstacles.
You will find that they haven't half the strength you think they have."**
...Inspirational Clergyman Norman Vincent Peale

Human Spiritual Powers

New short-term goals replace old ones when original goals are met or discarded. You don't have to complete shorter-term goals to start longer-term goals.

- *Short term goals (1-3 years)*
    - *Get a good job.*
    - *Save a three to six-month emergency fund.*
    - *Go on a great vacation.*
    - *Learn a particular language*
- *Medium term goals: (3 to 10 years)*
    - *Complete a desired level of education.*
    - *Start your own business.*
    - *Buy a new chariot.*
- *Long-term goals: (10 years to a lifetime)*
    - *Become a better person through character development.*
    - *Have and raise several good children.*
    - *Own your own hut and property free of debt*

Set your intent and focus it with courage, willpower and resolve on the results you wish to achieve.

- *Think often about success and what you can do to bring it about. Recognize, but **don't dwell on**, the problems and obstacles.*
- *Take the step-by-step **physical action** necessary to realize your goals.*
- *You can enlist the awesome power and energy of **Intention** and **Commitment** to help bring forth the results you desire by remaining committed and engaged until your goals are attained.*

"Commitment is a gift you must give yourself."
...Author Price Pritchett

- ***Intention*** and **commitment** *are the spiritual engines of creation. They are a power that helps keep successful people positive and creative in the face of negativity and disappointment.*

- *The **creative power** of your mind is designed to **focus** on the things that **you decide** are of the most importance to you.*

Reticular Activating System - *A bundle of cells called the reticular activating system or RAS lies at the base of your brain to sift, sort and evaluate the roughly 400 billion bits per second of incoming signals from all your sensory organs[5].*

- *The RAS evaluates everything you see, hear, touch, taste or smell to determine what needs your attention and what does not.*

- *Usually, the only three things that are permitted access to your consciousness are things that **threaten** you, things of **value** to you and things that you would consider **unique** or unusual.*

- *The RAS is activated by clear intention and commitment that signals it to adjust its filters and sends it hunting and sorting through your full array of experiences for whatever might help you with the implementation of your clearly identified intentions and commitments.[6]*

- *When tempted to think of fear or failure, put them out of your mind (lest they set the filters of your RAS searching for validators of your fears) and focus on positive scenarios and visions of success.*

- *The disciplined ability to keep control of your thought process is a crucial key to success.*

Resolution - *Intention and commitment can be focused with the power of a resolution, which can be the directing and impelling force in individual progress.*

*When you make a resolution, it means you are dissatisfied with your condition and intend to do something about it to produce a **better piece of workmanship** from the mental and spiritual materials of which your character and soul are composed.*

- *A resolution is no light thing, impulse or vague desire, but a solemn and irrevocable determination not to rest or cease from effort until the purpose of your resolution is met.*

- *None of us can change the way life works, but we can resolve to **understand how it works**, so that instead of complaining and fighting blindly against it, we can **grow** through what we **go** through in the **flow** of the established laws of life.*

*James Allen noted that when you **understand the process** of the transformation of your spirit and soul, you will accept life's challenges and difficulties knowing that **only by learning to pass properly through them** can you gain spiritual strength, maturity and peace.*

10. The Power of Forgiveness - *Harmful, destructive or sinful behavior by one human being will frequently have an adverse effect on other people.*

- *As a victim, you can and should take the appropriate steps for redress if available.*

- *However, if you maintain ongoing resentment, hatred or other ill feelings toward the perpetrator, it will serve only to retard your own spiritual development.*

Your ill will can be cleansed and released through the power of forgiveness. Every bit of condemnation, unforgiveness or fear we carry in our spirit is a wall between us, other people and God.

- *The extent to which we can measure spiritual progress is the extent to which we are getting rid of hatred, criticism and condemnation and filling our souls instead with unselfish and undemanding care.*

- *Forgiveness requires that you make a conscious decision to forgive your attackers by purging negative feelings toward them and praying that they can repent and get spiritual control over their actions.*

**Those who cannot forgive others
block a bridge over which they themselves must pass.**
...Confucius

- *There is much greater spiritual benefit to the **human doing** the **forgiving** than there is to the guilty ones being forgiven.*

- *The spiritual power of forgiveness can prevent negative behavior by one human being from creating a chain reaction of negative self-defeating feelings and behaviors in others.*

Professor Crozier recalled that Mahatma Gandhi, India's great spiritual leader, once said forgiveness is the attribute of the strong for the weak can never forgive.

In turn, Carter recalled that noted spiritualist Caroline Myss has said that when we harbor negative emotions toward others or even toward ourselves, we are slowly poisoning our physical and spiritual systems.

- *We can become emotionally toxic and bring that toxin into all of our relationships. We can become diseased from "carrying strife" with us for too long!*

- *Forgiveness is the antidote for toxic grudges and contaminated feelings. Unfortunately, we can learn to forgive only by being wronged.*

- *To maintain bitterness toward someone is like swallowing poison and hoping the other person will die from it.[7]*

11. <u>The Power of Patience</u> - *Patience is a first-rate power that will put the promises of God within your reach. It's a spiritual force that will make a winner out of you by allowing you the strength to think before you act and to overcome the pressure of circumstances that may be rushing you to wrong choices.*

Patience is the capacity to accept or tolerate delay, trouble, or suffering without getting angry, upset or giving up. Patient faith gives our spirits the time necessary to grow in a relationship with divinity. Patient courage allows us endure tough circumstances while keeping our spirits calm enough to hear from God.

"To forgive is to set a prisoner free and discover
that the prisoner was you!"
...Lewis B. Smedes

12. <u>The Power of Courage</u> - *The quality of mind or spirit that enables a person to face difficulty, danger or pain. There are two types of courage: physical courage and moral courage. Physical courage refers to the ability of an individual to face physical danger at risk of bodily harm. Moral courage is a test of character. It is the courage to take action or refrain from action for moral reasons despite the risk of adverse consequences. The spiritual Power of Courage includes both.*

The power of Courage enables us to be brave and willing to do what should be done even when afraid. It's not the absence of fear, but the ability to overcome fear. Sometimes it is the power to do what is right when everyone around you is pressuring you to do what is wrong. The power of Courage gives strength in the face of pain or grief. Living righteously with all its challenges takes a great deal of moral courage. Courage doesn't always roar. Sometimes it is the quiet voice at the end of a difficult day, saying I will try again tomorrow.

Staring fear in the face and powering through it with the powers of faith and courage is heroic work. Courage does not accept defeat; it does not surrender until all hope whatsoever is lost. Since Faith preserves hope, Faith and Courage together are an extremely valiant force nearly impossible to defeat.

III. Summary

Upon completion of the manuscript translation Carter and the Professor take a break and reflect back on their accomplishment.

"Carter, do you know what this whole manuscript is?" asks Dr. Crozier.

"Brimming with enthusiasm, the professor says, "Why, this amounts to nothing less than a powerful operating outline of the human soul!

Getting carried away and practically dancing with passion, he adds, "It's an absolutely incredible gift from the ancient past that may be from God himself. It's, it's priceless."

In a voice growing louder by the word, the rotund old professor declares, "Given its age, language and the location where it was found, this could have been written with divine guidance by King Solomon himself!"

Chapter 4 Spiritual Powers

Ending with a dramatic crescendo of grandiloquence he adds, "It applies more than ever to humanity today, and I, James Warren Crozier, with your assistance, have translated it from behind the shroud of obscurity into the full view of a modern world in desperate need of it!

Calming down, Professor Crozier says, "What I found to be the most profound and insightful passage was that 'only by learning **to pass properly through our challenges and difficulties...**' That must mean learning to handle these things in the right way spiritually during the tempting and stressful experiences of human life."

Carter agrees saying, "That's pretty weighty stuff alright; yet it seems reasonable when you think about it. It makes me think of people as sculptors chiseling a statue with every blow **shaping the sculptor** as well as the sculpture."

"So, we are reminded again," adds Carter, "that just reading and studying the ways of the soul are not enough; if our soul is to make progress, we must be able to apply the guidelines properly in the lived experience of life with all its ups and downs, challenges and difficulties."

Professor Crozier says, "All my life I have struggled to surmount the challenges and obstacles in my life with fear, worry and stress because I did not understand this simple truth. I see that I must continue to apply myself to them, **but to do so realizing that they are not there to defeat me, but to help me learn to overcome them** by making sometimes tough choices with **faith**, **patience** and **self-disciplined courage**."

This translation also provides the answers I have been seeking to the vital question about human spiritual powers exclaims Carter. The old professor remembering Carter's spiritual quest then asks to see the journal about the human soul Carter had mentioned previously. Being greatly impressed with it, he then asked if he might be allowed a copy of the handbook upon its completion.

> **God did not give us a spirit of timidity,**
> **but a spirit of power and love and self-control.**
> *...2 Tim 1:7*

The answer to question three is the summary of this chapter:

HUMAN SPIRITUAL POWERS

Human Spiritual Powers

The following dozen spiritual powers, **when properly used and understood,** *can help fulfill our spiritual destiny and the proper transcendence of our souls by giving us tremendous authority over the challenges of human life.*

1. *The Power of Faith*

2. *The Power of Imagination and Positive Imaging*

3. *The Power of Prayer*

4. *The Power to Choose*

5. *The Power of Self-discipline*

6. *The Power of Thought*

7. *The Power of Confession and Repentance*

8. *Power Projection and Confirming Action*

9. *The Power of Intention and Commitment*

10. *The Power of Forgiveness*

11. *The power of Patience*

12. *The Power of Courage*

Carter says his favorite phrase is "Salvation is not a matter of escaping the flesh as much as it's a matter of **properly inhabiting it**. One goal of the soul is self-control, and the **physical body and the physical world are circumstances that oblige us to learn self-control**."

Carter commented that the wisdom of each point seems self-evident once it is understood, yet they are not nearly so obvious beforehand.

"It is truly remarkable how long it might take each human being wandering around in a no man's land of spiritual ignorance to stumble across even one of these truths for himself, if indeed he ever would," said the professor.

**When you decide to walk by faith, you don't get rid of trials.
You just learn to handle them better.**
...Pastor Kenneth Copeland

Chapter 4 Spiritual Powers

"And you are right Carter; once revealed they seem so obvious as to be self-evident. In fact, the first paragraph we translated referred to them as simply evident. Truly, I guess these dozen spiritual powers have been hiding in plain sight all along."

Keeping Joseph Wright and his family in the picture each step of the way, they publish the translated works in relevant academic journals. As a result, they are able to contract on the father Ahmed's behalf to sell the original manuscript to the foundation of a large well-known museum for a handsome sum of money.

With Joseph's permission, Carter discusses the entire manuscript with his grandfather who thinks it the most unique and perceptive list of spiritual powers, laws and principles ever put together. They are unique he says because of the way these points of well-known information are described, combined and revealed to be spiritual powers, laws and principles of great significance.

Joseph and his family are thrilled to be so suddenly and completely lifted out of poverty by the old manuscript. Later they invite Dr. Crozier and Carter to their new home anytime they can come for a vacation to the holy land.

Carter's parents relay a message from Zach that he and the doctor are doing well although APOLLYON has twice more tried to disrupt the doctor's speeches. Carter updates Zach on his status and the fact that he is still trying to determine if joy and happiness are a way to his soul.

With the answer to the third question of the quest complete, Carter is now ready to move on in search of the answer to question number four of the six most essential and enduring questions of all time:

WHY SUFFERING IN EVERY HUMAN LIFE?

The account of **Living as a Modern Soul in a Human Body** continues in Book 4 *"Why Human Suffering"* where Carter learns about the nature of human suffering and evil in a hard way.

I slept and dreamed that life was beauty.
I awoke and found that life was duty.
...*Transcendentalist Poet Ellen Sturgis Hooper*

Human Spiritual Powers

The famous image of humankind struggling to move forward the great wheel of human progress by increasing virtue, knowledge and wisdom; the spirits of which fly above

Select verses of the poem
"Raphael" by John Greenleaf Whittier circa 1822[8]

We shape ourselves the joy or fear
of which the coming life is made,
and fill our future atmosphere
with sunshine or with shade

The tissues of the life to be
we weave with colors all our own,
and in the field of destiny
we reap as we have sown.

Whittier, the famous poet said, "We are born selfish. The discipline of life develops the higher qualities of character, in a greater or lesser degree. It is the conquering of innate selfish propensities that makes the saint; and the giving up unduly to selfish impulses that makes the sinner."

---

[1] James Allen, *Above Life's Turmoil p.16* - Dualism is the middle of three stages in the development of the soul that is still partly based in the animal stage of sensory pleasure, but is also aware of the third stage of spiritual knowledge.

[2] Ibid, p.46

[3] Ibid, p.31

[4] From a sermon by Pastor Harold Massey

[5] Arntz, Chasse and Vicente, *What the Bleep Do We Know*, p46

[6] Price Pritchett, *The Unfolding*, Chapter 5

[7] Bob Welch, *52 Lessons from "A Christmas Carol" (by Charles Dickens)*

[8] John Greenleaf Whittier; The Complete Poetical Works of John Greenleaf Whittier; Houghton, Mifflin Company; 1894

Appendix 1
Five Steps to Faith
and Dealing with Doubt

Developing and sustaining faith is an ongoing process that requires time and commitment. Choosing to side with God through faith is a continual challenge. It's not something you do once and it's done. It's an extended continual process of choosing to believe and act with faith.

1. Make a willful **choice** to believe. It takes a serious decision to start up the road of faith for it is a long road. For most of us, it's not a simple parking spot where illumination strikes all at once. This great journey, like all others, starts with the critical first step: the **choice** to learn how to believe in God by reading the bible, meditation and Prayer.

2. Go where faith grows, where you hear it discussed and see it practiced: houses of worship, spiritual events and religious media stations. Faith increases by hearing the Word of God preached or read.

3. Read scriptures and other faith building materials. Faith comes by reading the Word of God. Make sure you are developing faith in the right things by studying the Word of God (The Bible).

4. Pray for stronger and stronger faith.

5. Start living like a person of faith, align your behavior more with that of faithful people. Live according to the principles and tenets of Godly conduct starting with the Ten Commandments, and pursue a **virtuous character**. Pray daily for God's help. Read books of prayer.

Doubt ever tries to overcome our growing faith, so expect it and don't be troubled by it; just stay on the road and tell your doubts, "I knew you were coming, but I am prepared to believe you not, so just keep going."

The measure of our faith is not to be found in our ability to completely avoid doubt but in our growing ability to dispel it. The stronger faith gets, the easier it is to dispel doubt when repeatedly it comes knocking as surely it will. We all have doubts from time to time.

A married couple best begins on the journey together for if one gets too far beyond the other, their beliefs and lifestyles begin to diverge, which can weaken their relationship.

The first steps are the hardest, because doubt and some of your own character traits will be at their strongest against you. If you push through and begin building faith, it will get easier eventually. Faith is harder to gain than to sustain.

"Take the first step in faith.
You don't have to take the whole staircase, just take the first step."
... Dr. Martin Luther King, Jr.

Appendix 1
Five Steps to Faith
and Dealing with Doubt

As you make your way along the road toward full faith and spiritual maturity, you should be able to make more of the following improvements in your character, which will in turn continue boosting your spiritual growth creating a virtuous circle in your life.

1. Becoming a better more respectable role model
1. Being morally pure and faithful to your spouse
2. Becoming more temperate in word and action
3. Becoming more prudent, wise and humble
4. Becoming more hospitable, unselfish and generous
5. Communicating better in a less threatening manner
6. Becoming sober and not addicted to substances
7. Becoming less self-centered and controlling
8. Becoming less quick tempered to anger
9. Becoming less argumentative, contentious or abrasive
10. Becoming more loving, kind and considerate
11. Becoming less materialistic and less concerned with possessions
12. Becoming a better spouse and parent
13. Caring more about what is good and Godly
14. Becoming more just, discerning and fair
15. Becoming more self-controlled and disciplined

Remember, the first step is simply to **decide** that you want to develop faith in the Divine power of God. It will then take prayer, study and perseverance and the will to ignore doubt along the way that will bring gradually the **golden mindset of faith**.

We must be willing to first believe, so that we may begin to understand because spiritual matters can be understood only by open minds willing to accept on faith some truths they don't yet comprehend.

However, a willfully obstinate soul with an intellectually rigid mind seeking only reasons **to doubt** will never be able to perceive the glorious dimension of spiritual reality. Therefore, open your mind and suspend your doubt lest you lock yourself out of your only avenue to eternal security.

"Unless you believe, you will not understand."
... Isaiah 7:9

Appendix 2 Delphic Maxims

In the year 550 B.C., Carter finds himself wearing a robe in ancient Greece over two thousand years ago, on his way to a famous Oracle to seek wisdom from the greatest clairvoyant of the time.

Located in the Temple of Apollo high on Mt. Parnassus near the Gulf of Corinth, in central Greece, is the **Oracle of Delphi**, famed throughout the ancient world for predicting the future.

The temple is well up on the southwestern slopes of the highest mountain in the region. Below the Temple, in the Valley of Phocis, a deep green river of millions of olive trees spreads and plunges from the mountains toward the sea.

Carter follows a winding path in a relentless climb up to the "Sacred Way" at Apollo's shrine. Upon arriving, he rests, pays a fee, is required to buy a sacrificial goat and undergoes a cleansing ritual before being admitted into the circular Tholos which houses the celebrated oracle.

The oracle, a priestess called the Pythia, is sitting on a high three-legged chair, in an ecstatic trance wearing a short plain white dress. She removes a veil revealing a radiant and beautiful expression and stares at Carter who nervously asks, "Will, will, I find my soul in happiness?"

She is holding laurel leaves and a dish of spring water into which she gazes. She inhales deeply of vapors, rising from a cleft in rock beneath her. Slowly her figure seems to enlarge, her hair stands on end, and her complexion changes from pink to a deep golden bronze. She begins panting, and slips into delirium. Finally, in a deep voice that seems inhuman, she utters, "Follow the maxims and happiness will follow you."

With his question only half answered, Carter dizzily falls asleep and awakens from the dream in his own bed. Remembering his dream, he determines to find the Delphic Maxims to which the oracle referred.

The Delphic maxims are in fact a set of 147 brief sayings that offer wise guidance to human beings. These pearls of wisdom were inscribed in the ancient Greek Temple of Apollo that housed the Delphic Oracle.

Most of those maxims as recorded on the next pages are still valid today. They along with the Ten Commandments, scripture such as the Book of Proverbs and other expressions of ancient wisdom suggest that despite thousands of years of human experience, we **have ever been** in need of the same guidance to address the **same persistent needs and weaknesses in our unchanging human nature.**

THE DELPHIC MAXIMS

Follow God

Obey the law

Respect your parents

Be ruled by justice

Know by learning

Listen and understand

Know yourself

Set out to be married

Know your opportunity

Honor the hearth

Be in control of yourself

Help your friends

Control your temper

Exercise prudence

Honor forethought

Do not use an oath

Embrace friendship

Pursue honor

Be eager for wisdom

Praise the good

Find fault with no one

Praise virtue

Practice what is just

Ward off your enemies

Exercise nobility of character

Shun evil

Be impartial

Guard what is yours

Shun what belongs to others

Listen to all

Be fair of speech

Look after your own

Nothing in excess

Save time

Look to the future

Despise insolence

Educate your young

If you have, give

Be aware of deceit

Speak well of everyone

Be a seeker of wisdom

Choose what is holy

Act from knowledge

Shun murder

Pray for what is possible

Consult the wise

Test your character

If you have received, give back

Look down on none

Make use of expertise

Give what you aim to give

Honor generosity

Envy no one

Be on your guard

Praise hope

Despise slander

Gain possessions justly

Honor good people

Control your marriages

Recognize fortune

Don't make risky promises

Speak plainly

Associate with likeminded people

Control your expenditure

Be happy with what you have

Revere a sense of shame

Repay favors

Pray for success

Listen and observe

Work for what you can own

Despise strife

Detest disgrace

Restrain your tongue

Shun violence

Use what you have

Judge incorruptibly

Make accusations face to face

Speak from knowledge

Have no truck with violence

Live free of sorrow

Have kindly interactions

Complete the race without fear

Deal kindly with everyone

Do not curse your sons

Be courteous

Respond in a timely manner

Struggle for glory

Act decisively

Repent of your errors

Control your eye

Give timely counsel

Act without hesitation

Guard friendship

Be grateful

Keep secret what should be secret

Pursue what is profitable

Accept due measure

Dissolve enmities

Accept old age

Do not boast about power

Shun hatred

Acquire wealth justly

Do not abandon honor

Despise evil

Take sensible risks

Never tire of learning

Never cease being thrifty

Admire oracles

Love those whom you rear

Do not fight an absent foe

Respect the old

Instruct the young

Do not put your trust in wealth

Respect yourself

Do not initiate violence

Die for your country

Do not live your life in discontent

Share the load of the unfortunate

Have no grief

Beget good from good

Make promises to none

Do as well as your mortal status permits

Do not put your trust in chance

As a child be well-behaved

As a youth be self-disciplined

As a middle-aged person be honest

As an old man be sensible

At your end be without sorrow

The prestigious Oracle of Delphi was the most famous diviner of the future in the ancient world from about 560 B.C. to A.D. 393 when it was destroyed by the Romans. It was built over a geological fault line that may have released hallucinogenic gases and was considered by the ancients to be the center or navel of the world.

The source of the historic Delphic Maxims is not certain. However, they have been attributed by early scholars to the **Seven Sages of Greece** who were among the wisest men of their time in the 6th century B.C. History records that these Maxims were inscribed on the columns of the temple of Apollo that surrounded the Delphic Oracle.

Actual Ruins of the Tholos, the circular structure housing the oracle Pythia
the famous **Oracle of Delphi** in the great temple of Apollo
high on Mt. Parnassus

Painting of the great Temple of Apollo at Delphi by Albert Tournaire

Author
James L. Cannon
Lt. Colonel U.S. Army (Ret.)

Mr. Cannon is a retired university vice president, a former economics professor and a former corporate manager.

Lt.Col. Cannon is a Vietnam War veteran, who has served in the U.S. Air Force and the U.S. Army. He was also an undercover intelligence operative and retired as a decorated Army Reserve Intelligence Officer with the Defense Intelligence Agency in Washington, D.C.

As a community leader, the author has been a successful small city mayor; a chamber of commerce president and has served on the governing boards of several public organizations.

The Colonel holds University of Virginia degrees in economics and foreign affairs; GTE marketing, management and technology degrees and is an honor graduate of the U.S. Army's Command and General Staff College and a graduate of the University of Kentucky College Business Management Institute.

The author is happily married with a beautiful wife, two children, two grandchildren, a dog and a small business. His interests include philosophy, metaphysics and economics.

The author may be contacted by email at soulsline9@gmail.com